THE CODYS OF WYOMING

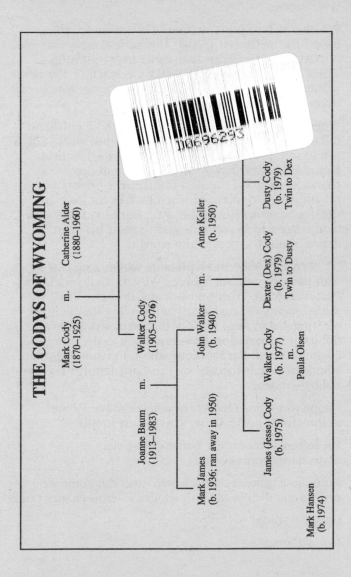

Mark Cody (1870–1925)   m.   Catherine Alder (1880–1960)

Walker Cody (1905–1976)

Joanne Baum (1913–1983)   m.   John Walker (b. 1940)

Mark James (b. 1936; ran away in 1950)

Anne Keiler (b. 1950)   m.

James (Jesse) Cody (b. 1975)

Walker Cody (b. 1977) m. Paula Olsen

Dexter (Dex) Cody (b. 1979) Twin to Dusty

Dusty Cody (b. 1979) Twin to Dex

Mark Hansen (b. 1974)

Dear Reader,

Whether rich or poor, no family is without conflict, including the Codys! *Dexter: Honorable Cowboy* is book 2 of Harlequin American Romance's new continuity—THE CODYS: THE FIRST FAMILY OF RODEO. I've never written a twin hero and I confess that Dexter is now one of my favorites.

When Josie Charles, the former high school girlfriend of Dexter's twin, Dusty, returns to Markton with Dusty's son in tow, fireworks explode between the brothers. Dexter believes Dusty, Josie and their son deserve a chance to be a real family—but Dexter's honorable intentions are challenged when he falls for Josie and decides he wants her for his own. But blood is thicker than water and Dexter struggles to resist his heart's desire…until Dusty sets him straight.

It's been an honor and a pleasure working on this series with talented authors Rebecca Winters, Cathy McDavid, Pamela Britton, Trish Milburn and Lynnette Kent. We shared plenty of laughs and hair-pulling moments as we struggled to keep track of the characters, plots and tidbits of information from one book to the next. And I want to thank our fabulous editor, Johanna Raisanen, who kept us gals focused on the Cody family's favorite hobby—rodeo!

I hope you enjoy *Dexter: Honorable Cowboy*. Be sure to look for his twin Dusty's book next month!

For information on my books please visit www.marinthomas.com.

For up-to-date news on Harlequin American Romance authors and their books visit www.harauthors.blogspot.com.

Happy reading!

Marin Thomas

Dexter:
Honorable Cowboy

Marin Thomas

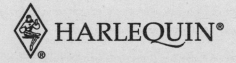

HARLEQUIN®

TORONTO • NEW YORK • LONDON
AMSTERDAM • PARIS • SYDNEY • HAMBURG
STOCKHOLM • ATHENS • TOKYO • MILAN • MADRID
PRAGUE • WARSAW • BUDAPEST • AUCKLAND

Recycling programs for this product may not exist in your area.

ISBN-13: 978-0-373-75318-5

DEXTER: HONORABLE COWBOY

Copyright © 2010 by Brenda Smith-Beagley.

This edition published by arrangement with Harlequin Books S.A.

For questions and comments about the quality of this book please contact us at Customer_eCare@Harlequin.ca

® and TM are trademarks of the publisher. Trademarks indicated with ® are registered in the United States Patent and Trademark Office, the Canadian Trade Marks Office and in other countries.

www.eHarlequin.com

Printed in U.S.A.

ABOUT THE AUTHOR

Marin Thomas grew up in Janesville, Wisconsin. She attended the University of Arizona in Tucson on a Division I basketball scholarship. In 1986 she graduated with a B.A. in radio-television and married her college sweetheart in a five-minute ceremony in Las Vegas. Marin was inducted in May 2005 into the Janesville Sports Hall of Fame for her basketball accomplishments. Even though she now calls Chicago home, she's a living testament to the old adage "You can take the girl out of the small town, but you can't take the small town out of the girl." Marin's heart still lies in small-town life, which she loves to write about in her books.

Books by Marin Thomas

HARLEQUIN AMERICAN ROMANCE
1024—THE COWBOY AND THE BRIDE
1050—DADDY BY CHOICE
1079—HOMEWARD BOUND
1124—AARON UNDER CONSTRUCTION*
1148—NELSON IN COMMAND*
1165—SUMMER LOVIN'
    "The Preacher's Daughter"
1175—RYAN'S RENOVATION*
1184—FOR THE CHILDREN**
1200—IN A SOLDIER'S ARMS**
1224—A COAL MINER'S WIFE**
1236—THE COWBOY AND THE ANGEL
1253—A COWBOY'S PROMISE
1271—SAMANTHA'S COWBOY
1288—A COWBOY CHRISTMAS

*The McKade Brothers
**Hearts of Appalachia

To my daughter, Marin

Congratulations on your high school graduation!
I'm so proud of all you've accomplished in and out
of the classroom. You have a bright future ahead of
you. Believe in yourself and never give up on
your dreams. As you head off to college this fall—
work hard, but make time for fun and
don't forget when you get the chance…DANCE!

Love, Mom

P.S. Dad says, "Go Otter!"

Chapter One

Stinky.

Two thousand pounds of mulish, malodorous stench.

Dexter Cody had drawn a rodeo bull famous for its rank smell and cranky disposition.

"Cowboy up!" Dexter's competitor hollered.

The setting sun cast long shadows of the cowboys gathered around the bucking chutes at the Sweetwater County Fair in Lander, Wyoming. Soon, the fairground lights would wash the arena in a warm glow, the oppressive July heat would ease and hooves would pummel the dirt along with a few unlucky cowpokes.

Adrenaline pumped through Dexter's veins and he cursed the protective vest preventing him from sucking in a deep breath. A trickle of sweat beaded at his temple, then dripped down his cheek as he and Stinky exchanged evil-eyed glares.

A quick glance into the stands confirmed that none of his siblings were in attendance. Good. Dexter didn't relish falling flat on his face in front of family. And if word got back to his mother that he'd ridden a bull—just for fun—she'd lop his head off. His dismal track record in the event didn't dampen his love for the sport. He wished he possessed half the talent of his older brother, Jesse, who excelled at bull riding. Instead, Dexter and his fraternal twin, Dusty, team roped together—which wasn't nearly as exciting as bustin' bulls.

Dexter didn't care to delve too deeply into his attraction to the widow-makers. At twenty-seven years of age, his bull-riding days—even for fun—were numbered. He limited his participation in the event to a few times a year—when he reached his limit of *pissed off.* This evening, thanks to his twin, Dexter's pissed-off tank overflowed. Most days he was content to toe the line and assume his fair share of responsibility for the Cottonwood Ranch working horses. But for the past month Dusty's habit of disappearing at the most inopportune times grated on Dexter's nerves.

A twinge of guilt pricked his hide. Dexter's sour mood wasn't solely the result of his brother's less-than-stellar work ethic. Dexter admitted his ornery feelings had intensified since his brother Walker had been a double winner at the Cody Roundup this past Sunday. Not only had Walker taken first place in the steer-wrestling event but he'd also landed a bride. Walker and his new wife, Paula, were a perfect match and their happiness only made Dexter more aware of the sad state of his own love life.

Shaking off the depressing thoughts, he inched closer to the chute. A whiff of bull schnocker shot up his nose. Good ol' Stinky had dropped a cow patty the size of a dinner plate.

"Ladies and gents, before we kick off America's first extreme sport we got a special treat for y'all. Trick rider Cheyenne Dakota's gonna do a little showin' off on her horse Belle."

Applause broke out when the beautiful cowgirl rode into the arena, her long black hair flying in the air. Dexter had run into Cheyenne at several rodeos through the years and the one time he'd attempted to strike up a conversation with her, she'd given him the brush-off. Not even Dusty, who had a reputation of charming the jeans off most women, had been able to cozy up to the full-blooded Native American. Cheyenne did a hand-stand on the back of her horse, then flipped upright and raced from the arena.

The crowd quieted and cowboys covered their hearts with their hats when the Barclay sisters took stage and belted out "The Star Spangled Banner" with a cowboy twang. Finally, heads bowed as the announcer prayed for the cowboys and the great United States of America.

Forcing his attention to the task at hand, Dexter climbed the chute rails and settled onto Stinky's back. The heat from the animal's body cooked the inside of his thighs as he worked the bull rope between the pinkie and index fingers of his gloved hand, clenching and unclenching the nylon.

"All right, folks, it's time for a little bull bustin'!" The crowd roared. "Y'all know these daredevil cowboys have to keep their seat for eight seconds if they're gonna have a chance at winnin' any money."

"Lookin' a might peaked, hoss." Dwayne Kettle wasn't any better at bull riding than Dexter, but the cowboy liked to believe he was.

"Just gettin' high on Stinky." Dexter sniffed the air, then frowned. "Or maybe it's you I smell." Nothing curled a nose worse than a cowboy's armpit soaked with fear.

"Ladies and gentlemen…turn your attention to chute number three. Dexter Cody is about to tangle with Stinky! Dexter's part of the Cody clan over there in Markton. His older brother Jesse's a contender for the NFR in bull riding. Let's see how Jesse's little brother does today."

"Ready?" The gate man nodded to Dexter.

As I'll ever be. When the gate opened, Stinky shot into the arena flinging Dexter side to side. He clamped his back teeth together and raised his right arm high into the air. Stinky swung his head and bull spit slapped Dexter across the face. *Shit.* Distracted, he lost count of the seconds in his head.

Not that it mattered. Stinky spun right, left, then right again in quick succession, catapulting Dexter through the air. He landed in the dirt. Hard. Instinct kicked in, and he rolled in time to avoid a stomping from Stinky's hooves. The bull fighters closed in to distract the enraged animal, but when Dexter crawled to his knees, Stinky charged.

The image of his mother crying at his funeral spurred Dexter to his feet. Just as he reached for safety, the bull's horns caught him in the seat, pitching him over the arena rails. For the second time in less than eight seconds, Dexter landed in the dirt.

"Best leave the bull ridin' to your brother." Kettle chuckled.

Shut up. Dexter spit dirt from his mouth. When the world stopped spinning, a pair of red cowboy boots came into focus inches from his nose. Then a feminine hand appeared before his face. He reached for the slim fingers with pink-painted nails and scrambled to get his legs under him. Once upright, his mouth sagged open.

"Josie?"

"Hello, Dex."

"Been a long time." Nine years hadn't left much of a mark on Dusty's former high-school sweetheart—the girl Dexter had secretly coveted. Josie's face was leaner, more finely sculpted, but her brown eyes were as big as he'd remembered. Her freckles, which he'd always been a fan of, had faded except for the smattering across the bridge of her nose. The strawberry blond hair was shorter—the locks brushing her shoulders. She wore a white Western shirt with black horses stitched across her small, perfect... He dropped his gaze from her breasts to the leather belt cinching her narrow waist.

"Better luck next time." Josie smiled a tad crookedly.

Dexter noticed he still held her hand and reluctantly released his grip. "I was sorry to hear about your father's heart attack." He wiped his shirtsleeve across his face, erasing any trace of Stinky's slobber.

"Thanks. The doctor restricted him to bed rest." Josie shrugged. "He's not cooperating, so I flew home to help Mom."

She motioned to the bull being loaded into the chute behind him. "I thought you and Dusty team roped together."

The mention of his brother's name dampened Dexter's enthusiasm at running into Josie. "We're still a team, but once in a while I mess around with bulls."

"I don't recall you being the daredevil type."

"There's a lot you don't know about me." Her eyes widened, and he silently cursed. He hadn't meant to sound defensive. "What's your father's prognosis?"

"As long as Dad takes it easy and remains on his meds he should be fine. But it'll be tough to keep him down for long."

Most cowboys and ranchers worth their salt were stubborn. Josie's father was no exception.

"Dexter Cody." A stranger approached, offering his hand. "Bud Masterson. I hauled my horse here from Montana. Was hoping you'd take a look at him."

Well, shoot. Dexter had forgotten he'd agreed to meet with the rancher today. Masterson had phoned earlier in the week asking Dexter to evaluate a wild horse he'd purchased from a government holding pen. The man's timing left a lot to be desired. Dexter turned to Josie. "Are you sticking around after the rodeo?" At her nod, he said, "I'll catch up with you later."

Masterson led Dexter across the fairgrounds to the livestock trailers. The rancher rambled on about the stallion, but Dexter's mind remained stuck on Josie. He hadn't seen a ring on her finger, but that didn't mean she wasn't involved in a serious relationship. He wondered if Dusty knew she was back in town.

"He balks whenever a human comes near," Masterson said.

Shutting the door on all thoughts of Josie, Dexter stopped a short distance from the trailer to observe the white stallion. The animal appeared docile, so he moved closer. Suddenly, the stallion stomped his hoof several times. The horse had caught Dexter's scent.

"When I asked around about trainers your name came up more than once," Masterson said.

Rogue horses had become a hobby for Dexter. He wouldn't call himself a horse whisperer but he had a connection with horses on a level most people didn't. "Where did they capture the mustang?"

"Near the Canadian border earlier this year. He was on his way to the glue factory when I rescued him."

The stallion's brilliant blue eyes revealed a wounded spirit. After living in the wild, the horse would rather die than be confined to a pasture the remainder of his years. "He wants to be free."

"If I turn him loose, they'll shoot him."

"Why?"

"He's got a nasty habit of wandering outside the herd management area and destroying private property." Masterson rubbed his brow. "After I brought him back to my ranch, he broke free and caused a car accident. Galloped onto the road in front of a minivan carrying two kids. Could have been a hell of a tragedy. Luckily the family escaped with minor injuries."

"He probably smelled a mare in heat," Dexter said.

"If I can't keep the stallion within the confines of my ranch, he'll have to be put down."

An animal this magnificent deserved a better fate. "Drop him off at the Cottonwood Ranch." No need to give directions. Everyone in the states of Wyoming, Montana and Idaho knew where the Cody family resided. "Tell Big Ben to put him in the round pen with the high fencing." Big Ben was second in command when Dexter and Dusty were absent from the horse barns.

"You sure you want to keep a wild mustang at your place? Hate to see him injure any of your animals or ranch hands."

Dexter had little choice. He didn't have time to travel to Montana and work with the stallion. If that wasn't reason enough to stay close to Markton, then Josie's sudden appearance was. "We've got plenty of room." The Cottonwood Ranch boasted almost six hundred thousand acres. "Shouldn't be a problem keeping the stallion separated from our horses."

"You're his last hope." Masterson removed a business card from his shirt pocket.

"He got a name?"

Masterson shook his head. "If you tame him, you get to name him, Mr. Cody." With a tip of his hat the rancher hopped into the truck and drove off.

Josie. Dexter's heart pumped hard as he made his way toward the carnival rides. His excitement at meeting up with Josie today didn't make sense. He'd had a crush on her in high school, then when Dusty beat him to the punch and staked his claim on Josie, Dexter had had to settle for being friends with her. Eventually, he couldn't stand to be around her and not have her for himself, so he'd ended their friendship Christmas break of their senior year.

You should have told her how you felt about her.

With conscious effort Dexter slowed his steps. He'd better get hold of himself before he did something he'd regret. Keeping his distance made sense. However, at the moment he didn't feel particularly sensible. Besides, Josie had worked her way beneath his skin years ago. She wasn't any ordinary sliver. Pulling her out would cost him a chunk of flesh.

Maybe she's changed.

Josie probably had—everyone matured over time.

The safest course of action would be to treat her like a treasured artifact—keep her tucked away out of sight. No muss or fuss when she packed her bags and left town.

What if this time she sees you as more than a friend? More than Dusty's twin?

Dexter ended the mental debate with himself as soon as Josie came into view. She stood in line at the popcorn stand. All havoc broke loose inside his chest when she smiled at him.

So much for keeping his emotions in check around the woman.

"Business all taken care of?" she asked.

"Yep." Half his business, anyway. The other half stood next to him. Josie's scent—a crisp, clean smell—sparked off another adrenaline surge. This time the blood rushed straight to his groin. Rampant teenage hormones had evolved into a grown man's desire. "How'd you manage to escape taking care of your father today?"

"Between you and me—" Josie blew out a breath, the action ruffling her wispy bangs "—I needed a break from Dad."

"When did you get back in town?"

"This past weekend."

He grinned. "You and your old man always did butt heads." While in high school, Josie had complained to Dexter that her father had tightened the reins on her because she was dating Dusty. Everyone within a hundred square miles of Markton had been aware of the animosity between Hank Charles and Dexter's father, John Walker—but hell if anyone knew why the two men detested one another.

"Mom kicked me out this morning before my bickering with Dad gave *her* a heart attack." Josie moved forward in line and Dexter eyed her fanny and slim legs.

"You don't look any worse for wear after all the arguing." What he really meant to say was that Josie was more attractive now than she'd been in high school—and back then he'd believed her the prettiest girl in the area.

She motioned to his face. "You broke your nose at least once since I last saw you."

That Josie detected a difference in his appearance had Dexter wondering what else she'd observed about him in high school. Back then he'd assumed she'd only had eyes for Dusty. "How's life on the West Coast?"

"Great." Her smile drew his gaze to her mouth. The shiny gloss covering her lips set off fantasies of slow, wet, deep kisses. When he made eye contact with her, a sizzling flash of heat sparked between them.

Before he lost his courage, he asked, "How would you like to go—"

"Mom! Mom!" A little boy wearing cowboy boots and a food-stained Western shirt skidded to a halt in front of Josie. "Mom."

Josie's a mother?

"What, honey?" She cupped the back of the child's head and the expression on her face reflected a mother's love.

"Can me and Aunt Belinda ride the Ferris wheel?"

Dexter noticed a tall, big-boned blonde hurrying toward them. "I can't keep up with the little stinker," the woman said, joining the group.

"Belinda, this is Dexter Cody. I went to school with him and his brother."

"Nice to meet you. I'm Josie's neighbor. I'm visiting her folks for a few days before I return to California." She shook Dexter's hand, then smirked. "That was a nasty fall you took earlier."

Leave it to a woman to remind a man of his failings. "I've taken worse tumbles."

"This is my son, Matthew." Josie set a protective hand on the boy's shoulder and turned him toward Dexter. "Matt, this is Mr. Cody. Grandpa's neighbor."

"Hi." Matt glanced up at his mother. "Can we go on the Ferris wheel now?"

Dexter clenched his hands into fists as he stared at the child's face—more specifically the dimple in the boy's right cheek. As if he'd been peppered with buckshot, every ounce of excitement and anticipation at seeing Josie leaked out, leaving him hollow inside.

"Belinda, if you wouldn't mind riding with Matt—" Josie coaxed her son toward her friend "—I'll catch up in a few minutes."

As soon as the pair walked off, Dexter asked, "Does Dusty know?" He couldn't imagine his brother keeping the first Cody grandchild a secret from the family.

"Not yet." Josie avoided eye contact.

Questions pummeled Dexter until he felt physically ill.

When?

How?

Where?

The kid couldn't be more than four or five, which meant...Dusty had hooked up with Josie in the not-too-distant past. Funny how his twin had neglected to mention it.

A second shock wave pulsed through Dexter as he struggled to come to grips with this sudden turn of events. He couldn't believe the young girl he'd known in high school would have kept such a secret from her son's daddy.

Déjà vu all over again. The moment Dexter was ready to make a move on Josie his brother had once again staked his prior claim.

"Do you intend to tell Dusty—maybe before the boy's eighteenth birthday?"

Josie winced and Dexter gritted his teeth to keep from apologizing. He hadn't meant to lash out, but he didn't feel like being cordial.

"Yes, I'd planned to—"

"When?" Dexter's brain insisted it was none of his business when and how Josie Charles spread the news about her and Dusty's son. But his heart screamed in frustration at the injustice of it all.

During high school he'd stood on the sidelines waiting for his chance with Josie, figuring his brother would tire of her and move on to another girl. When that hadn't happened, Dexter had been compelled to avoid Josie.

Looks like you'll still have to keep your distance.

"Dusty has a right to—"

"I'll take care of it." Josie's mouth pressed into a thin line.

Tired, sore and raw on the inside, Dexter glared at her. "If you don't tell him, I will."

Chapter Two

Josie eyed Dexter's backside as he swaggered across the fairgrounds toward the parking lot. She tracked his black Stetson until the throng of fairgoers swallowed him whole.

Drat. This hadn't been how she'd planned introducing Matt to the Codys. Dusty deserved to be the first to know he had a son before anyone in his family.

Dex won't say a word.

Dexter... Although she'd dated his twin in high school, she and Dexter had been in several classes together and had gotten along well. They'd engaged in heated debates over the novels they'd read in Mrs. Wilson's American Literature class and they'd teamed up in Biology to present a report on cell osmosis. Whenever she'd wished to partake in a serious discussion she could count on Dexter's thoughtful insight and commentary. And then for reasons still unknown to Josie, Dexter suddenly distanced himself from her their senior year. Twice she'd gone out of her way to ask what she'd done to upset him, but he'd brushed off her concern and continued to avoid her. No one, not even Dusty, knew how deeply Dexter's cold shoulder had hurt her.

He wasn't cold toward you a few minutes ago. As a matter of fact, Dexter had been downright friendly, even eyeing her figure when he thought she wasn't aware.

Speaking of figures…Dexter had added several pounds of muscle to his frame since his teen years, and his stride conveyed purpose and confidence. She'd always believed Dusty had been the better-looking of the twins, but Dusty had never given her heart palpitations like Dexter's blue-eyed once-over after his bull ride earlier.

Don't even think about it, Josie. Reconnecting with Dexter during her stay in Markton was out of the question. She didn't trust him not to try to persuade her to make concessions where Matt was concerned—allowances she had no intention of granting. In order to prevent Matt from becoming a tug-of-war object she had to keep her guard up around all the Codys. She sucked in a deep breath to clear her brain of any lingering pheromones from Dexter's presence and made her way toward the Ferris wheel.

Josie had no one to blame for her current predicament but herself. She'd agonized over informing Dusty about her pregnancy, putting off the decision until after Matt was born. Then when she'd brought Matt home from the hospital she'd fabricated more reasons not to contact Dusty. Weeks turned into months and months into years and in the end it was Matt who took the decision out of her hands.

Two months ago her son had walked out of their apartment in the middle of the night in search of his father. For as long as she lived, Josie would never forget waking in the wee hours of the morning with the feeling that something was terribly wrong. When she'd checked on Matt and discovered his bed empty, panic threatened to consume her. She'd raced out the front door shouting Matt's name, waking her neighbors. She'd found him a few minutes later sitting at the corner bus stop with his backpack and teddy bear.

Matt needed his father, so Josie had begun making plans to bring her son back to Markton. Her father's heart attack had fast-forwarded those plans, and whether she was prepared or not, the time had come for Matt to meet Dusty and the rest of his Cody relatives.

Although she'd had her reasons—reasons she'd believed were legitimate—she was ashamed that her fear had denied Matt a chance to bond with his father. She couldn't give Matt those four years back, but she was determined to do everything in her power to ensure his relationship with Dusty was a positive one.

The Codys were one of Wyoming's most powerful, wealthy and influential families. If she wasn't careful how she handled the situation with her son, John Walker, the Cody patriarch, would make her life miserable. Josie's father had had firsthand experience tangling with his neighbor and Josie knew J.W. wouldn't think twice about using underhanded methods to gain an advantage where his grandson was concerned.

She arrived at the Ferris wheel as Belinda and Matt reached the front of the line. Josie waved and her son's sweet smile brought an ache to her throat. No matter that sleeping with Dusty had been a mistake, she'd always be grateful for the joy and love Matt brought into her life.

"You ridin' or what, lady?" asked the man standing next to her. A cigarette with two inches of ash at the tip wobbled between his lips.

"Sorry." Josie stepped aside so the man and his daughters could move forward in the line. With each rotation of the Ferris wheel, Josie's stomach knotted tighter. Deep down she worried the Codys would threaten her relationship with Matt. She had a career and a life in Santa Monica. How in the world would she and Dusty figure out a visitation schedule that worked for everyone?

Josie didn't expect or deserve empathy from Dusty's family, but she'd hoped Dexter might be her one ally in the Cody clan. Judging by his stunned expression upon discovering his twin had fathered her child, she doubted Dexter would stand in her corner. Besides, his loyalty would demand he try to convince her to return to Wyoming and raise Matt in Markton.

And Markton was the last place Josie wanted to be.

"HEY, DEX!" AT THREE O'CLOCK on Sunday afternoon Dusty was just showing his face around the barns—after the horses had already been fed and exercised. As usual Dusty's Border collie, Track, was by his side.

"What's the matter with Digger?" Dusty stopped outside the stall where Dexter examined the horse's front left hoof.

"Not sure." Dexter wasn't in a congenial mood. Ever since he'd run into Josie he'd slept in snatches each night, tormented by dreams of her and Dusty standing before a preacher saying "I do." Today he'd slipped from the house before dawn for an early-morning ride before Jesse and their younger sister, Elly, had risen for the day.

"The Missoula Hoedown's right around the corner. Is he gonna be okay by then?"

Why the heck did Dusty care? His brother had hardly been around to practice these days. "Digger'll be fine." Dexter patted the neck of his nine-year-old quarter horse.

"What's up with the stallion in the round pen?" Dusty grinned. "Is Mom breeding mustangs now?"

"Horse belongs to Bud Masterson from Montana. He rescued the animal from a government holding pen. Said he'd have to put him down if I can't take the wild out of him."

"If anyone can bend a horse to their will, it's you."

"We'll see." Dexter closed Digger's stall door.

"Heard you fell flat on your face at the fair in Lander."

News traveled fast between small towns in Wyoming—nothing better for cowboys to do than rodeo and gossip. "Don't say a word to Mom."

"Your secret's safe with me."

Speaking of secrets... "Got any plans for the rest of the day? Big Ben could use help training the yearlings."

Dusty snapped his fingers. "That's what I came out here to tell you. Josie Charles is back in town. She phoned a few minutes ago. I'm meeting her at the Spotted Horse for a beer. Want to come?"

Dexter wouldn't mind witnessing his brother's jaw drop when he learned he was a daddy. As soon as the uncharitable thought entered his brain, Dexter regretted it. He and Dusty had had their differences in the past but they were brothers and Dexter figured Josie's news would shake up his twin—not to mention change

Dusty's life forever. This predicament had been bound to happen sooner or later—Dusty's wild ways with women had finally lassoed him. The fact that the woman was Josie was a bitter pill to swallow.

"You go on without me. I've got to work with the stallion." Dexter left the barn, Dusty and Track dogging his heels.

"I can tell Josie another time if—"

"No."

Dusty grabbed Dexter's arm and tugged him to a stop. "What's wrong?"

He and Dusty were so close they often sensed when something was bothering the other one. "Nothing. Why?"

"Most of the time you tell me to quit screwing around and pitch in more."

"Yeah, well, today I'm in a good mood."

"If this is your good mood, I'd hate to be downwind of your bad mood."

"Beat it." Dexter shoved his brother.

Dusty chuckled. "Make me."

Aw, damn it. His twin loved a good scuffle. The problem was Dusty usually beat him, but right now Dexter was irritated enough by Josie's secret that he feared he'd pummel the crap out of his brother if they wrestled.

"Tell Josie I said hello." As Dexter walked off he called over his shoulder, "You planning to practice team roping before the Missoula rodeo?" Pinning Dusty down was like trying to catch a tumbleweed—you couldn't.

His brother waved him off as Track raced ahead and jumped into the bed of Dusty's truck. "Later!" Dusty shut the tailgate, then drove off.

"Where's he goin'?" Slim joined Dexter outside the barn.

"He's meeting a friend in town." Dexter headed for the mustang, which had been set free in a pen with ten-foot-high fencing. A mustang's main instinct was flight and the horses were notorious for trying to escape their enclosure.

The forty-eight-year-old ranch hand tagged along after Dexter, his right boot dragging against the ground. The retired rodeo clown's foot had been stomped on by a bull, causing nerve damage. The injury had ended Slim's career and triggered a ten-year drinking spell. Dexter had felt sorry for the short, skinny man and offered him a job working with the Cottonwood Ranch horses—on the condition Slim gave up the bottle. Four years had passed and the cowboy had yet to fall off the wagon.

Slim spit a stream of tobacco juice at the ground. "That stallion's a mean son of a bitch. Damned horse almost bit Big Ben yesterday."

Both men stopped at the pen and propped a boot on the lower fence rail. The stallion remained at the opposite end, ignoring his visitors. "J.W. know you brought that mustang here?" Slim asked.

"Nope." Dexter had intentionally kept his father in the dark about the new four-legged guest. A few months ago he'd approached the old man about his desire to train rogue horses in addition to managing the ranch's working horses. His father had nixed the idea, insisting Dexter had enough on his plate. A phone call had interrupted the conversation—rather argument—and nothing had been settled.

"Guess I'll mosey along and let you get on with yer whisperin'. Ricky and I are gonna work the lunge line with Brown Sugar and Sweet Pea."

Once Slim disappeared inside the barn, Dexter moved closer to the horse and made eye contact.

"I'm feeling penned in, too, big guy."

It wasn't that Dexter didn't appreciate his upbringing and the opportunities his parents' wealth afforded him and his siblings, but like the mustang, there were days when he felt the need for more running room. He loved working with the ranch horses, but his responsibilities along with rodeoing left little time for much else—including personal relationships.

The last time Dexter had been involved with a woman, the affair had ended in disaster. That was six months ago. He'd met Shannon a year ago at a rodeo when she and her horse had almost run him down during a barrel-racing event. They'd begun seeing each other as often as their rodeo schedules allowed, and it wasn't long before Dexter knew he was ready to settle down and start a family with Shannon. He'd proposed, but Shannon kept changing the wedding date. He'd suggested Vegas—just the two of them. No family. Shannon had agreed. They were both competing in rodeos the second weekend in January and had planned to hop separate flights to Vegas. Dexter had arrived first and had waited at their hotel, but Shannon had missed her flight. Then she'd missed the next one and the one after that. When she hadn't arrived by late Sunday afternoon Dexter knew he'd been stood up. He'd flown back to Markton, and the following week Shannon's engagement ring had arrived in the mail.

Seeing Josie yesterday and learning that the girl he'd once wanted for himself had had a child with Dusty—a guy who wasn't ready to settle down and didn't want to be a father—had cut Dexter to the core.

And of course there was Walker. His brother had recently returned from Iraq, and hadn't been looking to marry or begin a family. He'd met Paula, a young widow with a two-year-old son. A short time later Walker ended up in Reno tying the knot.

Damn it. Dexter had never felt more lonely than he did at this moment.

The stare-down with the mustang continued—neither horse nor man giving ground. The stallion's fear was palpable.

"Hungry, hoss?" Dexter said softly.

Ears perked.

Slim had left a bucket of feed next to the pen, so Dexter emptied the grain into the bin attached to the rails. The horse's nostrils flared, but instead of moving forward he backed away.

"Gonna hold out for a while, big guy?"

The horse neighed.

"Might as well see whose stubborn streak is stronger." Dexter pulled up a stool, sat with his back against the pen and practiced his rope-tying skills. He had all the time in the world to wait.

And to wonder how Dusty was taking the news he was a father.

JOSIE SAT INSIDE the Spotted Horse Saloon at a table in the back, away from the bar and sawdust-covered dance floor. Several cowboys had nodded in her direction when she'd entered the honky-tonk, but she hadn't recognized any of their faces—not a surprise since she'd made a habit of avoiding her hometown. Her mother loved the glitz and glamour of Hollywood, so her parents traveled to the L.A. area twice a year to visit her and Matt.

The population of Markton had grown by a whopping thirty-six people in the thirteen years Josie had been gone. The sign at the edge of town boasted 997 residents. Add Walker Cody's new wife and son and the town was one body short of the thousand mark.

Josie knew from experience that kids raised in rural towns got into trouble out of boredom. She'd been grounded a time or two for sneaking out her bedroom window in the middle of the night and driving off with Dusty to party with their classmates. The local teens congregated along the banks of the Greybull River, which ran through the Cody ranch. Dusty had introduced her to beer at the age of sixteen.

The memory made Josie smile. When Dexter discovered Dusty had coaxed her to drink, he'd become furious. The twins had almost gotten into a fistfight. Looking back on those days, she realized that Dexter had acted as protector whenever he'd believed Dusty was out of line with her. She wished more than ever that Dexter could protect her and Matt from the rocky road that lay ahead of them.

Josie had nothing against small towns but there was more to life than partying, rodeoing and ranching. She worried her son had inherited Dusty's rodeo genes. Already, Matt was begging his grandpa to teach him to ride a horse and throw a rope. Rodeo was a dangerous sport and few cowboys made money at it—even fewer were happily married. Look at Dusty—he'd mentioned he was still single when she'd phoned him to arrange their meeting.

You're still single, city girl.

Her situation was different. She had Matt. Josie didn't have time to date or hang out in bars picking up men. Unlike Dusty, these past four years she'd carried the weight of a huge responsibility—Matt. The word *responsibility* reminded her of Dexter. As long as she'd known him he'd juggled the demands of family, work and school without breaking.

The sound of the saloon door banging against the wall startled her. In walked Dusty. He grinned—the gesture wide, playful and a tad cocky—the same smile she'd fallen prey to in high school. Nerves tied in knots, she stood and braced herself.

He stopped at her side and opened his arms. She squeezed his rib cage. She was anxious—fearful of the price she'd have to pay for keeping Matt a secret. Dusty kissed the top of her head. "Aren't you a sight for sore eyes," he said.

Relieved when none of the old feelings she'd once harbored for the cowboy resurfaced, Josie wiggled loose. Because he was Matt's father, he'd always hold a tender place in her heart, but she was more certain than ever she didn't love Dusty.

"You look great." He flicked her hair. "Lost about six inches since I last saw you in California." He nodded to the empty glass on the table. "What are you drinking?"

"Diet Coke."

He frowned. "No rum?"

She shook her head. "But get yourself a beer." *You'll need one. Or two. Maybe three.*

"Did your friend make her flight this afternoon?" Dusty asked when he returned with their drinks.

"Yes." Josie had mentioned that she had to drive Belinda to the Yellowstone Regional Airport in Cody to catch the first leg of her flight to California.

Silence stretched between them.

When had talking to Dusty become difficult? He'd always been a conversation hog—filling up dead silences with "Hey, guess what?" and "I did this." Or "I'm rodeoing here." In high school their chats had focused on him and rodeo. Josie hadn't minded. Back then Dusty had been her world.

"Before I forget, Dex says hello."

That Dexter hadn't told Dusty about running into her and Matt in Lander didn't surprise Josie. Dexter was a stand-by-his-word kind of guy—he'd said he'd allow her a chance to tell Dusty first and he'd meant it.

"How's your dad?" Dusty asked.

"Grumpy. The doctor banned him from working around the ranch for a few weeks."

"Chores are always more fun when someone tells you not to do them."

Josie bit the inside of her cheek to keep from smiling. When they'd dated, Dusty had always found ways to avoid work in order to hang with her or his friends. "I was glad to hear Walker returned safely from Iraq. Mom said he's married now."

"Her name's Paula. She's got a two-year-old son, Clay. Mom and Dad are thrilled they finally have a grandchild."

Wait until J.W. and Anne Cody found out they had a biological grandchild. That was bound to be important to Dusty's parents.

"There's something I need to tell you." Josie counted on Dusty's good-natured optimism to kick in after she dropped the proverbial bomb.

"Bad news?"

"That depends on how you feel about being a father." She held her breath until her lungs pinched.

Dusty frowned and stared at her—a quizzical expression on his face. Seconds ticked by, then his eyebrows inched upward until they disappeared beneath the brim of his cowboy hat. His lips moved but no sound escaped his mouth.

Stomach churning, she said, "His name's Matthew. I named him after my mother's father. He's four and a half years old."

"When I stayed with you in L.A.?" Dusty asked in a hoarse whisper.

"Yes."

He squeezed the beer bottle until his knuckles turned white. "Why?"

"Why what?"

"Why have you waited four and a half years to tell me I have a son?" His sharp tone was so un-Dusty-like that she jumped inside her skin.

If she told him she feared his family would use their power, influence and money to try and take Matt away from her, Dusty would believe she was crazy. Josie's father knew all too well that when J.W. set his mind to something, nothing and no one got in his way. "I believed I was doing what was best for everyone involved."

"How is keeping Matt a secret from me in my best interest?"

"I don't love you, Dusty. And I know you don't love me." That he didn't protest confirmed her assumption about his feelings for her.

"Since when does a man loving a woman have anything to do with a father's rights?"

"I live in California. You live in Wyoming."

"And?"

"I knew your parents would coerce you into marrying me."

"No one forces me to do anything." Dusty dropped his gaze. "Marrying me would have made you miserable?"

"Marrying would have made both of us miserable." She smiled, because if she didn't, she'd cry. "You're a fun-loving guy, Dusty. You mean well. You want to do the right thing. But when it comes down to being a father, you're not ready and I had to protect Matt."

"Protect him from what?"

"From getting hurt." She rushed to explain. "Matt needs more from a father than a few hours of his time when he's passing through town on his way to the next rodeo." She paused, giving Dusty a chance to refute her statement. He didn't.

"Whether I'm ready to be a dad or not has little to do with my right to know I had a son out there in the world."

Her eyes burned. "I'm sorry."

"Is he here in Markton with you?" Dusty glanced toward the saloon doors. She wouldn't blame him if he ran. Her news had changed his life forever.

"Matt's at the ranch with my parents."

Dusty guzzled the remainder of his beer, then thunked the bottle against the table. "If you hadn't returned to Markton because of your father's heart attack, would you have told me?" he asked, his voice quiet but controlled, with a trace of cold condemnation.

"Actually, I had made up my mind to contact you before my father's heart attack."

"Why?"

"Matt ran away looking for you."

"What do expect from me?" At the steely glint in Dusty's blue eyes, Josie's bravado wavered.

She sympathized that he'd been caught off guard by the news he'd fathered a child, but it saddened her that so far he hadn't shown any curiosity about Matt. "I'm not asking anything of you. Matt and I are happy and content in California. As soon as my father's back on his feet, we'll return home."

Dusty's flat stare gave no indication if he was relieved or distressed by Josie's proclamation.

"What have you told Matt about me?"

"That you travel a lot and can't be with us." She winced at how pathetic the explanation sounded.

"You got the traveling part right." Dusty scooted his chair back.

"Where are you going?"

"Canada."

He was leaving the country? Okay, so she'd blindsided Dusty with the news he was a father, and yes, she imagined he needed time and space to absorb the shock, but Josie was angry and hurt on Matt's behalf that Dusty didn't intend to meet his son before he skipped town.

"I'd already arranged to take a few horses I trained up to Alberta to be used in a film," Dusty said.

Stunned that he appeared determined not to allow Matt or anyone to interfere with his plans, she mumbled, "I didn't know you trained horses for movies." He'd never mentioned the hobby when they'd met up in L.A. four years ago. Instead, he'd claimed he'd been in town on Cottonwood Ranch business.

"I'm a man of many talents," he said, a hint of the old Dusty shining through. "I'd appreciate you waiting to tell my folks about Matt until I return."

Selfishly she preferred to inform the relatives as soon as possible, deal with the fallout and then move on. But Dusty deserved a say in when and how the news about Matt became public. "Dexter already knows. We bumped into each other at the rodeo in Lander."

Dusty's blue eyes flashed. "Then tell my brother to keep his mouth shut, would you?"

For Matt's sake she had to give it one more try. "Don't you want to meet your son before you leave?"

Dusty pretended great interest in the tips of his boots, and Josie's heart dropped to her stomach. As she suspected—Dusty wasn't ready to make Matt a priority in his life.

"I'll speak to him when I get back," he said.

"And when will that be?"

"I don't know, Josie." His clipped tone warned her to back off.

"Fine. I won't say a word to Matt, my parents or anyone else until you're ready."

"I'll be in touch." With purposeful strides Dusty left the bar.

Josie pulled in a shaky breath. She prayed Dusty would come to terms with being a father soon, because she wouldn't breathe easy until she and Matt returned to California.

Chapter Three

"Honey, where's your brother?" Anne Cody asked when Dexter answered the phone Monday morning.

"Which brother?" He poured himself a second helping of coffee. He'd downed his first cup at 5:00 a.m. when he'd helped Paco feed the horses.

"The brother who's always missing," his mother snapped. "I tried Dusty's cell but his mailbox is full. That boy never checks his messages."

"Hang on one second." Dexter moved the phone away from his mouth and hollered down the hallway off the kitchen. "Hey, Elly! You know where Dusty is?"

"Sure don't!"

"Did you hear that, Mom?"

"Yes. What about Jesse?"

"He's meeting Nicki for breakfast in town, then he's heading out to her dad's ranch to take a look at a new bucking bull." Nicki Sable's father owned and operated the Sable Livestock Company, which provided stock for rodeos across the West.

"Did you try the phone in Dusty's apartment?" His twin lived above the horse barn, where he had more privacy to entertain the ladies. Dexter, Elly and Jesse shared the old homestead while their parents lived in the new showcase estate they'd built three miles away—as the crow flies. Walker, Paula and Clay lived in the small log cabin Grandfather Cody had built in the 40s up on Carter Mountain.

Dexter glanced out the kitchen window and scanned the ranch vehicles parked helter-skelter around the driveway. "Dusty's truck's not here." After learning he was a father, his twin had probably tied one on last night and was sleeping it off somewhere. Sympathy pricked Dexter's side. He'd be damned upset, too, if he'd been informed he was a father—four years after the fact.

Obviously his brother hadn't told anyone in the family about his *big* news, otherwise their mother would be pummeling Dexter with questions about Josie and Matt. "Want me to give Dusty a message if he shows his face around here anytime soon?"

"Tell him one of his rodeo twits keeps phoning the main house looking for him."

Figures. Dusty never gave out his cell number to the buckle bunnies who dogged him on the circuit. "Got it."

Before he disconnected, his mother asked, "What are your plans today?"

"Bill Chester's coming out this afternoon to take a look at Digger's front leg." Dr. Bill had taken care of the Cottonwood Ranch animals for years.

"I hope it's nothing serious." She cleared her throat. "I suppose you don't intend to tell me about the mustang you sneaked onto the ranch."

Crap. Nothing ever slipped past his mother.

"You'd better keep that rogue horse away from the breeding barn and Mr. Lucky Son." Anne Cody had worked tirelessly through the years to develop a first-rate quarter horse breeding and training facility on the Cottonwood Ranch. The famous stallion, Mr. Lucky Son, served as the foundation bloodline for his mother's breeding program and had been a gift from Dexter's father for her fifty-fifth birthday.

"Don't worry. I won't let the mustang mess up your horses' pedigrees."

"See that you don't, young man. Love you." Click.

Love you, too, Mom.

"What did Mom want with Dusty?" Elly waltzed into the kitchen, carrying her treasured camera. His younger sister by two years was a gifted photographer and several of her ranch photos were on display in an art gallery near Cody.

"Some buckle bunny keeps calling the house."

"I don't know why Mom won't give out Dusty's cell number." Elly tugged on her cowboy boots, her blond ponytail falling forward over her shoulder.

"Because Mom always protects Dusty. He's her favorite." Dexter and Elly exchanged knowing grins.

"Maybe, but I'm the favorite Cody cowgirl." Elly helped herself to a cup of coffee. "Dusty loaded his horses in a trailer and drove off around 3:00 a.m. this morning."

"Did he take Track with him?" Dusty and that Border collie were inseparable.

"Yep."

"Why didn't you say as much when Mom asked about Dusty?"

"Because Dusty made me promise not to tell anyone." She blew across the top of her mug.

Dexter quirked an eyebrow. "Then why are you telling me?"

"I'm terrible at keeping secrets."

"What were you doing awake that early in the morning?"

"Working on my blog for the ranch Web site." Elly frowned. "Dusty seemed troubled."

His twin had good reason to be upset. Still, how could Dusty just up and leave for God knows where and ignore the fact that he now had a son? "Did he say when he'd return or where he was headed?"

"Nope. Dusty's not in trouble, is he?"

That depended on how one viewed the situation. Because he had no idea how long his brother would be on the run, Dexter figured he'd better pay a visit to the Lazy S Ranch and check in on Josie and his nephew. Find out if she had plans to tell his folks about Matt.

That's a crock full of bull. You just want to see Josie, period. Dexter ignored the voice in his head and set the half-empty coffee mug in the sink. "Gotta run."

"Where are you off to?"

"Errands." No sense advertising his whereabouts when Elly admitted she couldn't keep a secret. Dexter crossed the ranch yard and stopped at the Equi-Ciser pen—a free run exerciser used to condition horses and drain their energy, enabling the animals to remain focused and calm during training sessions. "Hey, Ben. I'm taking off for a while."

Big Ben nodded. There was no one Dexter trusted more with the horses than the quiet man in his midfifties. Ben had been with the Cody ranch for over twenty years and had taught Dexter all he knew about training and handling cutting horses.

"I put in a call to the vet about Digger. If I'm not back by the time Dr. Bill shows up, phone me on my cell."

"Sure thing, boss."

Long ago he'd insisted that Ben call him by his first name, but the ranch hand refused. He knew his place in the chain of command.

Instead of taking the main ranch road to the highway, Dexter drove along a service corridor that cut through ranch land containing the Cody gas wells. The shortcut shaved ten miles off the trip. Twenty minutes later he pulled into the yard at the Charles ranch. Hank's pickup was the lone vehicle in front of the house.

Where were the hands? Other than the four horses penned in the corral next to the barn, the place appeared deserted. He was halfway to the house when he heard his name. Josie waved from inside the barn.

Switching directions, he veered toward her. "Morning." He tipped his hat out of habit and to keep his fingers occupied so they wouldn't be tempted to brush at the reddish-gold strands of hair plastered to Josie's sweaty face.

Her eyes flicked between him and the main house. "What are you doing here?" The question was accompanied by a rush of air as if she couldn't catch her breath.

"You okay?"

"Shoveling horse patties is a bit more strenuous than my yoga class." Her crooked smile zapped his body like a live wire.

"You shouldn't be mucking stalls. Aren't there any cowboys working the Lazy S?"

The sparkle in her eyes dimmed. "Not a one."

What the heck? "Why not?"

She moved farther into the barn and he followed her. Not even the dimly lit interior concealed the structure's deteriorating state. Dexter noted a million little things that needed repair or replacing. Hank Charles didn't seem like the kind of man who'd let his property fall into disrepair.

Josie pushed a wheelbarrow with a flat tire down the barn aisle.

"Let me." He nudged her aside and parked the barrow next to a stall. Then he removed the pitchfork from her hand. While he mucked, Josie spread fresh hay across the floor of the stall she'd already cleaned.

After a few minutes, she broke the silence. "Turns out my father's health is worse than I'd been led to believe the past few years, and he's racked up a pile of medical bills."

"What kind of health problems?"

"Dad has an irregular heartbeat on top of clogged arteries. Along with the stents he had put in, he's using a pacemaker and none of those things prevented his heart attack."

This was the first Dexter had heard of Hank Charles's worsening health.

"Dad's prideful. He wouldn't want anyone to know he's struggling to make ends meet."

Dexter wondered if his father knew their neighbor had hit upon hard times.

Josie rubbed her hands on her jeans. "Anyway, the reason Dad suffered a heart attack was because he'd worked himself into the ground after letting the ranch hands go."

Cursing under his breath, Dexter flung a horse turd into the wheelbarrow. No way in hell would he stand idle while Josie exhausted herself with chores, caring for a son and an ailing father. "I'll send over a few Cottonwood hands to help." Pride be damned. Neighbors stuck together in times of need.

"Thanks for the offer, but don't bother. Dad's sold off most of the herd. All that's left are the horses and fifty head of cattle grazing in the south pasture."

Josie didn't need his help, so why did Dexter feel the urge to butt in where he wasn't wanted? "The money my brother owes in back child support would more than pay the salary of a few cowboys."

"Oh, no," she protested. Sweat droplets ran down her face, leaving muddy tracks in their wake. Her ponytail hung askew and her damp T-shirt clung to her breasts.

All Dexter could think about at that moment was how sexy she looked. "What's wrong with neighbors lending a helping hand?" He forced the question from his dry mouth.

"Nothing, except—" Her eyes widened, then she turned her back, pitching more hay into the stall.

"Except what?" he asked.

"Never mind."

He would not be deterred. "Never mind what, Josie?"

"Money is the last thing Dad would ever accept from a Cody."

"It's no secret our fathers don't like each other, but they've been neighbors for over thirty-five years. That counts for something."

"You'd assume so, but Dad's got good reason to hold on to his grudge." The stubborn tilt of her chin dared him to bully her into confessing more.

"Then your father will just have to control his animosity for a few weeks while I help out. Besides, he's in no shape to throw me off his property." Josie let the subject drop and they worked in silence.

Holding his tongue wasn't easy for Dexter. He fought the urge to inquire about her talk with Dusty at the Spotted Horse Saloon. Even though it was none of his business Dexter wanted to know every frickin' detail—like when she and Dusty were going to marry and become a real family.

Hell. *She has a right to know the father of her son split.* Dexter set the pitchfork aside. "Dusty's gone."

She remained silent, pouring grain into the feed bag attached to the side of the stall.

"Elly said he loaded his horses into a trailer and drove off at three in the morning." Dexter watched Josie's body language, waiting for a sign that his twin's disappearance mattered to her, but she kept right on working.

Finally Josie spoke. "Dusty's on his way to Canada."

At least his brother had had the courtesy to tell Josie his destination.

"He's delivering the horses he trained for a film that's being shot in Alberta," she said.

Training horses for the movies—no wonder his brother hadn't been around much to help Dexter with the ranch horses. "Did he say when he'd return?"

"No."

Dexter jabbed the pitchfork into the soiled hay, wishing the prongs were piercing his brother's backside. "Are you okay with Dusty skipping town?"

"Sure."

"You shouldn't be."

A heavy sigh drifted over her shoulder. She wiped her hands against her jeans, then crossed her arms. "What's bugging you?" she asked.

"I'll tell you what's bothering me." He whipped off his hat and ran his fingers through his hair. "My brother learns that he has a son—you did tell him, didn't you?"

"Yes."

"Dusty finds out he's a father and instead of owning up to the responsibility, he splits." Dexter flung his arms wide. "My brother should be here, helping you with chores. Taking care of his son." *Taking care of you.*

Josie grasped his arm, her touch warming his skin. "Stop being so tough on Dusty."

Tough? Was she kidding? If someone didn't ride herd over Dusty, he'd never learn to put others before his own interests.

"Everyone can't be like you." She softened the criticism with a smile.

"What do you mean, like me?"

"You're the most responsible, hardworking man I know."

That didn't sound like a compliment.

She released his arm. "In fact, I find you very intimidating."

"Why?"

"Because you always do the right thing. You play the game of life straight up. You never cheated on a test in school. You never lied to the teacher or made up excuses if you didn't do your homework."

"Since when is being ethical and truthful a bad thing?"

She laughed, the high-pitched giggle flustering him. "Those are admirable qualities." Her smile faded. "But by rarely making mistakes, you've set the bar too high."

Not true. He'd made a whopper of a mistake in high school when he hadn't challenged his brother for Josie's affections.

"I'm just saying that you're a tough act for Dusty to follow."

"That doesn't excuse him from his responsibilities and—"

"Dusty's not avoiding responsibility." She set her hands on her hips, and Dexter hated that she appeared determined to defend his twin.

"Then what do you call running off to Canada?"

"Don't you have a tiny bit of sympathy for your brother? He just found out he has a four-year-old son. He needs time to absorb the shock and figure out how best to tell your parents. As soon as he returns we plan to break the news to both families."

Guilt kicked Dexter in the gut. He admitted he might be coming down too hard on Dusty, but damn it, why did his brother have to go and get *Josie* pregnant? Why couldn't it have been another woman—a woman Dexter hadn't had feelings for?

"So your folks don't know Dusty is Matt's father?"

"No. From the beginning I've told my parents that Matt's father didn't want to be involved in our lives."

Dexter's chest tightened. He'd kept Josie Charles on a pedestal since high school and for some stupid reason he was disappointed in her.

You're disappointed because you hold everyone up to your standards. Just like Josie said—you think you're perfect.

Was it true? Did others feel the same way about him? Was that why Shannon had gotten cold feet at the last minute and left him at the proverbial altar in Vegas—because she'd felt she couldn't live up to his expectations?

"You're not ticked off at Dusty for leaving?" he asked. Maybe Josie was being easy on his brother because she felt guilty for keeping Matt all to herself for years.

"To tell you the truth, I thought Dusty took the news well."

Dexter scoffed.

"Some men—" her eyes narrowed and Dexter got the feeling she was referring to him "—would have been angry, resentful and might have threatened to take my child from me."

He'd never do anything like that—would he? "Did Dusty meet Matt before he left?"

"No." Josie pitched clean hay into the next stall as if she were flinging a baseball. Maybe Dusty wasn't totally off the hook with her after all.

If Dexter had been in his brother's shoes no one and nothing would have prevented him from meeting his son.

"Mom! Mom!"

At the sound of Matt's voice, Josie walked toward the front of the barn, glad for the interruption. Dexter possessed the ability to both frustrate her and turn her on at the same time—maybe because she found all that *responsibility* and *commitment* darned appealing.

"In here, Matt."

"Grandpa wants to know why—" Matt skidded to a stop in front of Josie. "Who's that?"

"Hello, Matt." Dexter moved closer to Josie, the air stirring with a hint of his cologne—musk and sandalwood. She resisted the urge to lean close and sniff him.

"I'm Mr. Cody." Dexter held out his hand. "We met at the rodeo a couple of days ago."

Matt's eyes rounded when Dexter's huge hand swallowed his. "You fell off Stinky."

Dexter laughed, the sound straight from the bottom of his belly. Josie couldn't remember hearing him laugh like that—not even when they'd joked during their lunch period in high school. "Are you ready to help your mom with chores?"

"What are chores?"

Dexter shot her a perplexed frown. So what if she wasn't one of those mothers who created chore charts and gave out sparkly stickers when her child picked up his toys. "Matt—"

"Can I help, Mr.—" Matt glanced at Dexter "—what's your name?"

"Dexter Cody. You can call me Mr. D, if you want."

"Can I help Mr. D do chores?"

"Honey, the barn's dirty and—"

"But I wanna help."

"I'll keep an eye on him," Dexter promised.

Matt's help would most likely create extra work for Dexter and delay his leaving the Lazy S, but Josie didn't have the heart to disappoint her son. "You can help

Mr. D while I check on Grandpa." She ruffled her son's blond hair. "You listen to Mr. D, young man, and do as he says."

"Okay."

Josie hurried to the house, hoping her father wouldn't make a big deal out of Dexter's appearance. She should have known better.

"You tell that Cody boy to get the hell off my property," greeted Josie when she walked through the front door. Her father's recliner sat by the window, allowing a bird's-eye view of the barn and the truck sporting the Cottonwood Ranch logo.

"That's not very neighborly, Dad."

"Exactly what I said." Josie's mother waltzed into the room with a glass of water. "Time for your pills."

"I don't need any more damned pills."

Phyllis Charles might be a petite woman and two inches shorter than Josie's five-foot-seven height but she had the temperament of a pit bull when riled. She set the water glass on the table next to the recliner, then pried her husband's fist open and slapped two pills on his palm. "Take 'em or I'll shove 'em down your throat."

Josie coughed to cover her smile. Her mom acted tough with her father, but Josie knew for a fact that her parents loved each other deeply and her father's heart attack had shaken her mother's world.

"Better not mess with Mom, or she'll burn your supper," Josie teased.

"Listen to your daughter, Hank."

Her father grumped but took the pills, then her mother leaned down and kissed his forehead before retreating to the kitchen.

"Since when did you get back together with Dusty?"

"I haven't gotten back together with Dusty. That's Dexter out in the barn." Her father had never been able to tell the twins apart.

"What's he doing here?"

"Cleaning horse stalls. We ran into one another at the rodeo last week and he asked how you were doing."

"I bet he did—bunch of vultures them Codys are. Buzzing around my ranch, waiting for me to kick the bucket so they can move in and take it all."

"Dexter is doing no such thing. He offered to help, nothing more."

Her father's face flushed. "I don't need help."

That was a lie, but no one discussed the possibility that her father's health might never recover enough to enable him to resume caring for the ranch. If that was the case, then her parents would have to sell and her father's worst nightmare would come true—John Walker Cody would end up owning the Lazy S.

Josie hugged her father. "Stop fretting. Things always work out the way they're intended to."

She questioned whether her words were meant to reassure her father or herself.

Chapter Four

"Is this good, Mr. D?"

Josie stood in the shadow of the barn door and tuned her ears to the conversation between Dexter and her son.

"Looks like you've got the hang of spreading hay, squirt. Are you sure you haven't done this before?"

"Nope. We don't got hay at my house."

Fighting a smile, Josie watched Dexter push the wheelbarrow to the horse stall at the opposite end of the barn. Matt trailed behind, flinging fresh hay every which way into the clean stalls.

"You don't have any horses where you live?" Dexter asked.

"No, but we got lots of dogs. My aunt Belinda has a dog and his name's Chocolate. But he bit me."

"Were you hurt?"

Matt shook his head. "I gotta time-out 'cause Mom said I wasn't supposed to take Chocolate's bone."

"Moms usually know what they're talking about."

Matt sat on a bale and picked at the straw. "Do you got a mom, Mr. D?"

"Sure do. Right now she's mad at me."

Her son's mouth formed an O. "Did you do something bad?"

"Sort of."

Intrigued, Josie inched closer, then dived behind a sack of grain in the corner.

"I brought a wild mustang to our ranch and my mother's afraid the stallion might cause a ruckus with the other horses."

"What's a wild mustang?"

"A horse that's never been ridden or handled by a human."

"Does he got a name?"

"Not yet." Dexter chuckled. "You sure do ask a lot of questions."

"Mrs. Patterson says if we ask lots of questions it means we're gonna be smart when we grow up."

"Who's Mrs. Patterson?"

"My teacher. Mr. D?"

"What?"

"Is your mom gonna make you sit in a time-out?"

Josie pictured Dexter sitting on a pint-size stool in the corner of his mother's kitchen and smiled.

"She just might make me do that, Matt, if the mustang doesn't behave."

"Mr. D?"

"You ever run out of air, kid?"

"I don't know, but, Mr. D? Do you got a dad, too?"

Josie held her breath.

"Yep. I have a father."

"Oh."

Josie peeked over the feed bag. Matt scuffed the toe of his boot against the ground. "I got a dad, but Mom says he's really busy."

"I bet you'll see your father real soon."

Matt shrugged his slim shoulders. "Maybe. But I gotta grandpa."

"Grandpas are special."

"Grandpa was gonna teach me how to ride a horse, but Grandma said no 'cause his heart's all banged up."

"Hearts are tricky things. Your grandpa might have to take it easy for a long time. But if your mom says it's okay, I'll give you a few riding lessons."

Panic swept through Josie. She couldn't let Matt take riding lessons at the Cottonwood Ranch lest one of the Codys recognize the resemblance between her son and Dusty. She intended to keep her promise to Dusty that they'd break the news to his folks when he returned from Canada. The alternative wasn't much better. If Dexter gave Matt riding lessons at the Lazy S, Josie's father would put up a fuss, which wouldn't be good for his heart. *Drat.* She wished Dexter would have discussed riding lessons with her first before Matt got his hopes up.

"I'm gonna tell Mom!" Her son jumped off the hay bale and dashed past Josie.

"You can come out now," Dexter said.

Figured the cowboy would catch her spying. She stood and brushed the dirt off her jeans. "You shouldn't make promises to Matt before checking with me."

Dexter removed his hat and wiped his shirtsleeve against his sweaty brow, the action reminding her that she'd forgotten to bring him a drink from the house.

"I didn't see any harm in offering a riding lesson since I'll be around helping with chores."

"Getting close to Matt right now isn't a good idea." She pulled a pair of wire cutters from her jean pocket and opened a bale. As much as she wished for her son to bond with his uncle, she worried that Matt might become too attached to Dexter and not give Dusty the time of day when he returned from Canada. No one could predict a child's reasoning or actions.

"I offered to teach him how to ride, not be his father."

Lord, she hadn't remembered Dexter being this stubborn in high school. *Let him do it, Josie.* What harm could come from a few riding lessons?

"I'd have to smooth things over with my father first."

His blue eyes flashed, drawing Josie's scrutiny. Their color wasn't the electric blue of Dusty's and Matt's but a paler hue with a greenish ring around the irises. Gazing into his eyes was like drowning in a moss-covered pond.

"I'll speak with your father," Dexter said.

"Thanks, but I'd better do the talking."

"As soon as I dump the soiled hay in the compost pile I'll see about the cattle."

Josie wanted to protest, but she hadn't checked the herd since her return to Markton. She'd been too busy entertaining Belinda and refereeing arguments between her parents. "I'll go along."

"Who'll watch Matt?"

She glanced at her watch. "It's almost time for lunch. Mom should be able to handle him for a little while." She walked off, calling over her shoulder, "I'll fetch us some drinks."

Instead of using the front door Josie walked around to the back of the house and stepped into the kitchen. Her father and Matt sat at the table. Her mother stood at the counter making sandwiches.

"What's this I hear about Matt taking riding lessons from a Cody?"

"Dad, I haven't got time to talk now." She opened the fridge and grabbed four water bottles. "Dexter and I are heading out to check on the cattle."

"The herd's fine," her father protested.

"When's the last time it rained?" she asked.

"Not long ago."

Josie glanced at her mother. "Going on twelve days now," her mom answered. "Yellowstone got a good soaking a while back, but the rain skipped over us."

Almost two weeks without rain meant the stock tanks would have only a few inches of water left in them at best.

"Be good for Grandpa and Grandma." Josie kissed Matt's head.

"Tell Mr. D I wanna ride a big horse."

"You'll ride whatever horse Mr. D thinks you should ride." Josie paused at the door. "See you later."

When she walked around the side of the house her heart stuttered at the sight of Dexter leaning against the hood of his truck. Arms folded over his chest, legs crossed at the ankles and a sliver of straw hanging from his mouth—the quintessential cowboy pose. Not once had thoughts of Dexter turned lustful in high school—all her hormones had been focused on Dusty. So how come she suddenly noticed the way Dexter's snug jeans fit at the crotch? The way his hands gripped a pitchfork? The way his muscles bunched across his shoulders when he pushed the wheelbarrow?

Knock it off, Josie. She had enough on her plate right now—she didn't need another serving of Cody cowboy.

Dexter opened the passenger-side door as she approached and she grinned.

"What?"

"That's the one thing I miss about Wyoming—old-fashioned cowboy gallantry." He shut the door and got in on the driver's side. She handed him a water bottle.

"Thanks." He downed the entire bottle before starting the engine. "So guys in California don't open doors for girls?"

"Not many of them."

"You said the cattle are in the south pasture, right?"

She nodded. Her father kept the herd there in the summer because the area sat in a basin beneath the Shoshone Forest where the cooler temperatures produced richer grazing grass. During the winter months the cattle remained near the homestead and their diet was supplemented with hay.

As the truck bumped along the service road, she asked, "What's Dexter Cody been up to since college?"

"Nothing as exciting as you having a baby."

"Have you come close?" she asked.

"To having a baby?" The corner of his mouth tilted upward.

She landed a playful punch against his shoulder. "You know what I mean. Have you come close to getting married?"

Dexter strangled the steering wheel. "Once."

"What happened?"

"Didn't work out." He'd gone to heck and back for Shannon, trying to keep their relationship solid. Between hopping commuter planes to watch Shannon barrel race all over the West, caring for the Cottonwood Ranch horses and competing in rodeos with Dusty, Dexter had worn himself into the ground. Looking back on that time now he realized how one-sided his affair with Shannon had been.

"I'm surprised." Josie's comment snapped him out of the past.

"Surprised about what?"

"I expected you to be married and have a couple of rugrats by now." She shrugged. "You're a rock kind of guy."

He chuckled. "A rock?"

"Yeah. A man a woman can depend on. A guy who'll always be there for her—a rock."

Secretly pleased Josie held him in such high esteem, Dexter's face heated at the compliment. *Don't puff up your feathers too much.* No matter how intriguing the possibility of getting reacquainted with Josie might be, the mother of his brother's son was off-limits.

If Dusty had any sense he'd marry Josie. A lot of people tied the knot for lesser reasons than having a child together. Besides, Josie and Dusty weren't strangers. They had a history together. They'd gone steady in high school—obviously that attraction hadn't faded if they'd conceived Matt.

Acting honorable, however, was more difficult than Dexter anticipated. At the moment, with Josie's sweet scent filling the cab, he wanted to lean across the seat and nuzzle her neck. Banking his sexual thoughts, he asked, "What made you settle in L.A.?"

"Right after high-school graduation I flew to California with Kristen Mobley. Remember her? Her father owns a convenience store in Cody." Josie waved a hand in front of her face. "Anyway, once I saw the City of Angels I knew I'd never live in Markton again."

The conviction in her voice surprised him. "You hated Markton that much?"

"I didn't hate Markton as much as I hated the idea of everyone knowing your business."

"Gossip makes life interesting." There were occasions he wished people would keep their opinions to themselves, but those times were few and far between. More often than not, nosiness was a person's way of showing they cared.

"When Mom and Dad offered to help pay for my court-reporting school I decided to remain in L.A. I got a part-time job, rented a small apartment with two other girls and never looked back."

If only Dexter could stop looking back—back to Josie and what might have been if he'd had the courage to ask her out before his brother had.

"Now Matt and I live in a large apartment community in Santa Monica. No one knows your business unless you tell them."

"What if—"

"I know what you're going to say." She huffed. "How will I know if a psychopath or serial killer moves in next door?"

Surely Josie would understand that his family would worry about her and Matt when they learned Matt was a Cody. "Well...?"

"Most people are murdered by an acquaintance not a stranger."

Touché. A year ago a woman in Cody had been shot by her husband during a domestic dispute. The husband had been sentenced to twelve years in prison.

"Have you ever considered living anywhere other than Markton?" Josie asked.

"Nope. I'm a die-hard cowboy." Why would anyone trade in paradise—Wyoming's crisp, clean mountain air and vast miles of wilderness—for smog and sprawling suburbs?

"There are times I miss the snowcapped mountains...."

He sensed a *but* coming.

"But I don't miss the long winter months and the spring blizzards that leave you stuck in the house for days on end."

"You might change your mind if you were housebound with someone...fun." Why hell had he said that? She'd think he was—

"Why, Dexter Cody...are you flirting with me?"

He swallowed a groan. "Damn."

"What's wrong?"

He slowed the truck to a crawl. "Break in the fence line." Lazy S cattle were nowhere in sight. Thank God for distractions!

"I hope they didn't wander onto Cottonwood land." Josie's teeth worried her lower lip and Dexter cursed again—silently. If his brain didn't stop putting a sexual twist on Josie's every word or action, he'd go nuts trying to behave himself around her.

"One way to find out." Dexter drove over a cattle guard and onto Cody land. Extracting fifty head of Lazy S cattle from twenty-five hundred cow and calf pairs would be a daunting task. "Maybe they're over the ridge." He drove another half mile, then hit the brakes. "We're in luck."

A small group of cattle followed by three cowboys crested a ridge and headed in their direction. Dexter made a U-turn and returned to Charles land, parking the truck several yards from the gaping hole in the fence.

"Is that Jesse riding up front?" Josie shielded her eyes against the sun's glare.

"Yep." Dexter could spot his older brother's white cowboy hat ten miles away. He waited as Jesse and the hands herded the cattle back through the opening in the fence, then he grabbed his tools and got to work repairing the barbed wire.

"Sorry for the trouble, Jesse," Josie said when Dexter's brother slid from the saddle.

"Josie Charles." Jesse removed his hat. This Cody brother wore his blond hair much shorter than the twins'. "Where have you been hiding since high school?" The infamous Cody blue eyes sparkled, then his expression sobered. "I was sorry to hear about your father's heart attack."

"Thanks. He'll be fine as long as he listens to his doctor and doesn't overdo."

"How long you in town for?" Jesse asked.

"Just until my father is back on his feet." The sooner she returned to Santa Monica the better. She'd had to take an unpaid leave from her job while her father recuperated and she worried about using the last of her savings to make the rent and pay bills if she needed to stay in Markton longer than a month.

"Fence is fixed." Dexter stowed the tools in the truck bed. "We're lucky you corralled them before they mingled with Cottonwood cattle," he said to his brother.

"Cows don't travel too fast in this heat." Jesse grinned.

"Mom says you're going all the way to the NFR this year," Josie said.

"Tell your mother I appreciate the vote of confidence. I'm gonna give it a hell of run, that's for sure." He motioned to Dexter. "Speaking of rodeos, where the heck has Dusty disappeared to? Slim said neither of you have practiced this past week."

Josie hid a smile behind a fake cough. Years ago Dusty had complained to her that Jesse took rodeo too seriously. The eldest Cody brother lived and breathed bulls and expected his siblings to devote as much time and energy to their events as he did to his.

"We'll get around to practicing, don't worry," Dexter said. "Digger's got a sore leg, so I'm resting him for a few days."

Jesse mounted his horse. "If you hear from Dusty tell him to call home. Some buckle bunny's trying to track him down and she keeps phoning the main house."

The words *buckle bunny* conjured up memories of Josie having to battle other girls for Dusty's attention. That was one aspect of their relationship she hadn't enjoyed.

"Don't be a stranger, Josie. Stop by the ranch. Mom loves showing off her prize stallion, Mr. Lucky Son."

The thought of paying a social call to Anne Cody before Josie and Dusty shared the news about Matt seemed wrong in every way.

Jesse shifted in his saddle, giving Dexter his full attention. "We tracked a cougar roaming the edge of the forest last week. You might want to move these slabs of beef closer to the homestead until the cat leaves the area."

"Thanks for your help," Josie said when Jesse signaled his men it was time to leave. "I'll make sure they don't stray again."

Once Jesse and his men left, Josie and Dexter got back in the truck. "Your brother won't tell anyone what happened today, will he?" The last thing her father needed was a confrontation with J.W.

"No need to."

Had Josie's father embellished the story of J.W. swindling him years ago? How could J.W.—as despicable as her father painted him to be—have raised five honest, hardworking kids?

Dexter drove southeast a quarter mile, then turned onto a dirt path. She wasn't surprised he knew the location of the water sources on her father's property. Ranchers needed to be familiar with their neighbors' spreads in order to lend a helping hand during tough times. The dirt road dead-ended and Dexter parked the truck. They hiked through underbrush to a small glen with a spring-fed pond. The water level was dangerously low. Good thing her father had cut the size of the herd.

"The spring that feeds this pond is drying up," Dexter said. "Your father's going to have to dig a well."

There was no money for a new well. "If I remember right, one of the stock tanks is on the other side of that hill." She pointed to a small knoll in the distance. They hiked to the tank—bone-dry.

"The cattle broke through the fence because they were looking for water," Dexter said.

"I imagine the other tanks are empty, too." She followed Dexter back to the truck and they made the drive to the Lazy S ranch house in silence, giving Josie ample time to contemplate her father's financial woes. When Dexter parked in front of the house, he said, "I'll be back tomorrow with a couple of hands to help move the cattle in closer."

"Don't bother," she said.

"What do you mean?"

"The cows have to take their chances with the cougar." And scarce water. "Dad doesn't have enough hay to supplement their diets and the pastures near the house have been overgrazed."

"It's none of my business, but if your father needs help, I've got money saved. I can float him a no-interest loan. Until he's back on his feet."

Josie didn't know whether to laugh at the absurdity of a Cody lending a Charles money or to weep at Dexter's sincere offer. After what she'd done to his brother—keeping Matt a secret—she didn't deserve his empathy or his generosity. "You're a true-blue cowboy, you know that." At his frown she explained. "You live by the cowboy code."

"What code?"

She smiled. "My mother's a Gene Autry fan. When I was in kindergarten she made me memorize his cowboy codes."

"How many of them are there?"

"Ten. The one that comes to mind right now…a cowboy must help people in distress."

Dexter scoffed and she smiled at his impatience. "A cowboy must be a good worker—you are. He must respect women, parents and his nation's laws—you do."

"You haven't been home in years. How would you know if I've broken a law or not?" he asked.

"A cowboy always tells the truth. And as long as I've known you, you've never lied."

"People change."

"Not you."

He grimaced.

"A cowboy must be gentle with children, the elderly and animals," she continued, amused by the rosy hue spreading across his cheeks.

"All right. Enough of the Gene Autry stuff. Tomorrow, I'll speak to your father about moving the herd."

"I don't remember bullheadedness being one of the codes." Her comment didn't budge his serious expression. She sighed. "I'll do my best to prepare him." She hopped out of the truck. "But, Dex. Don't go overboard. Okay?"

"Promise. Tell Matt as soon as I get your father's cattle squared away, I'll give him his first riding lesson."

She considered protesting but figured Dexter would throw one of the cowboy codes back in her face. "Okay." She watched until the truck disappeared in a cloud of dust.

What was it about those good-looking Cody men? She'd better keep her guard up around Dexter. She'd already succumbed to Dusty's charm and look where that had landed her.

Dexter's different. He's solid. Dependable.

And he broke off your friendship without a word of explanation. If she was smart she wouldn't give Dexter the chance to hurt her again. She hurried toward the house, realizing what was missing from her perfect life in Santa Monica—a good old-fashioned cowboy.

Chapter Five

"About time you called," Dexter grumbled into his cell phone early Tuesday morning. "Mom's pissed that you took off without telling her." The least his twin could have done was inform their parents of his plans before skipping the country.

"I need you to do me a favor," Dusty said.

The word *favor* sent up red flags in Dexter's mind. "No favors. I've got my hands full with that damned stallion, nursing Digger's leg and—"

"You saying Digger won't be ready for the Missoula Hoedown?"

"What do you care? You haven't been around to practice."

Dusty cursed. "I called to ask if you'd keep an eye on Josie and Matt until I return."

The mention of Josie's name sucked the steam out of Dexter's mad.

"I'm—" Silence ensued and Dexter envisioned his twin tunneling his fingers through his hair. "—still trying to wrap my head around everything, you know?"

No, Dexter did not know.

Have some compassion. He's your brother. "Then what are you doing in Canada when Josie and your son are here in Markton?"

"I signed a contract. I'll be home as soon as they finish filming the scenes with my horses."

Dexter hated asking the question, but he needed to know Dusty's intentions toward Josie—especially after Dexter discovered the old feelings he'd once possessed for her hadn't completely died. "Any thoughts about you and Josie and the future?"

"I'm weighing my options," Dusty answered after a heavy pause.

If his brother had no desire to tie the knot with Josie, Dexter would be free to...*what?* He'd had a huge crush on her in high school and when Josie had chosen Dusty over him, he'd been devastated.

You never gave Josie the chance to choose, you idiot. You never told her how you felt about her.

None of that mattered anymore. Josie was Dusty's girl—back then and even more now. Dexter's feelings for her didn't matter. His loyalty belonged to his brother, and he'd do whatever Dusty needed him to do. *Sounds like you're spouting one of those frickin' cowboy codes Josie talked about.* Had Gene Autry's insides ever twisted like a pretzel when he followed his codes?

"To my way of thinking, bro, you've got only one option." *Marriage.*

"This isn't just about me. Josie gets a say, too," Dusty said.

"No matter what happens between you and Josie, nothing's going to change the fact that you're Matt's father."

A string of four-letter words blistered Dexter's ear. He'd pushed his brother too far. "Josie's a big girl," Dexter said. "She doesn't need a babysitter." Cowboy code be damned—the less time he spent with Josie the better for all concerned.

"If Josie or Matt asks for anything would you make sure they get it?"

Matt needs a father. Want me to step in and take your place? As soon as the thought entered his mind, Dexter felt a pain shoot through his intestines and figured he'd end up with an ulcer by the time the dust settled between Josie and his brother. "I'm helping them out as we speak."

"What do you mean?"

"Were you aware Hank Charles cut his herd to fifty head?" Dexter asked.

"Why so few?"

Dexter's thoughts exactly—why bother owning cattle at all. "Hank's had a run of bad luck." If Josie wanted Dusty to know more about her father's health problems, she could tell him. "The Lazy S herd crossed onto Cottonwood land the other day looking for water. Jesse found them before they mixed in with our cattle."

"Anyone tell Dad?"

"Heck, no." No sense stirring up trouble between the old men.

"You haven't told anyone about Matt, have you?" Dusty asked.

Since when had Dexter ever given his twin a reason not to trust him? Guilt filled Dexter, adding to the pain in his midriff. If his brother knew some of the untoward thoughts Dexter possessed about Josie, Dusty would call upon another brother to keep an eye on her and Matt. "I gave you my word I wouldn't mention Matt to anyone."

"Good. And thanks for helping Josie's dad."

Someone had to do it, and as usual Dusty wasn't around.

"Anything else?" Dexter wanted off the phone. Talking to his brother was detrimental to his health.

"Nope, that's all I called to say."

"Some rodeo queen keeps phoning the big house asking for you. She's driving Mom nuts."

"That's Roxy. She'll give up eventually."

Before he suggested Dusty tell his harem of bimbos he was no longer available, the dial tone buzzed in Dexter's ear.

"Ready, boss?" Slim hovered ten feet away.

How much of the conversation had the ranch hand heard? Good thing Slim wasn't a talker. "Is the water-tanker truck ready?"

"Yep. Paco and Ricky loaded a trailer with a week's worth of hay."

"Give me ten minutes with the mustang—" Dexter glanced at his watch. "—then we'll leave." He headed for the round pen.

This morning the stallion didn't bolt when Dexter approached. Progress. Man and mustang engaged in a stare-down. "You better behave while I'm gone." The horse neighed. "Later today I'll introduce you to the lunge line."

The animal's ears perked. "You won't like the exercise," Dexter warned the horse, then lost himself in the stallion's blue eyes—eyes that begged for freedom. He wished he could trade places with the animal.

Dexter would be far better off if someone penned him in and kept him away from Josie Charles.

DEXTER EYED THE LAZY S BARN in the distance as he led the caravan of trucks up the gravel road. He didn't expect Hank Charles to welcome his help this morning, but he hoped Josie had been able to convince her father to keep out of the way and permit Dexter to go about his business rounding up cattle.

He stepped on the gas as the truck climbed a rise, then slammed on the brakes when he reached the top. Josie's father stood dead center in the middle of the road. "Shit." He shifted the truck into Park and hopped out.

"Mornin', Mr. Charles." He stopped a few feet away. The imposing man Dexter had remembered from his youth had deteriorated into a shrunken coot. Heart problems had left their mark on the once-robust rancher.

"Josie says you're gonna—" Hank's breath came fast and hard "—bring the cattle in closer." The quarter-mile walk from the main house had taxed the old man.

Choosing his words carefully so as not to upset Josie's father, Dexter said, "My brother Jesse spotted a cougar up on the ridge last week. The cat's been hunting in the area awhile. Got one of Simms's ewes a few days ago."

"Serves Simms right. Damned sheep don't belong in cattle country."

Dexter fought a grin. "Your herd will be safer if we get them out of the valley."

"The pastures near the house have been grazed to the ground."

"Figured that might be the case. I brought enough hay for a week."

"Thought of everything, have you?" The wrinkles around Hank's eyes deepened.

"Just being neighborly."

"Since when does J.W. give a hoot about his neighbors?"

Taken aback by the comment, Dexter was speechless. What would the old man say when he discovered his daughter and Dusty had a son together? Only a matter of time before a Cody and a Charles walked down the aisle. "If you won't accept Cody help for yourself, then do it for your wife and your daughter." He nodded into the distance where the two women stood on the front porch of the ranch house.

"Darned females are nothing but trouble." Hank's shoulders slumped.

In an attempt to salvage the old man's pride, Dexter said, "I'll make a deal with you, Mr. Charles."

"What kind of deal?"

"I've got a wild mustang at our ranch and my mother wants the horse gone yesterday."

"What's your mustang got to do with me?"

"I need a place to train the horse without distractions."

"You want to bring the mustang here?"

"Your round pen's got a high enough fence to keep him from escaping. What do you say I board the horse at the Lazy S in exchange for helping out with your cattle?"

Now that Dexter had made the offer he wanted to yank it back. What was he thinking bringing a wild mustang to the Lazy S? Dexter had no business being anywhere near Josie—not when he couldn't keep his feelings in check. And if Josie wasn't reason enough to rescind his offer, then the fact that he wouldn't be around all the time to keep Matt away from the stallion was. Hank Charles was in no shape to intervene if the horse escaped the pen.

"Deal," Hank said.

"I'll remove the mustang if he becomes a threat. You have my word." Dexter held out his hand and Hank stared at it.

"The Cody word ain't worth nothing, son, so don't waste your breath."

Ignoring the testy comment, Dexter said, "Hop in. I'll give you a lift back to the house." They rode in silence. Dexter parked near the porch, then Hank muttered a "Thanks" and got out.

Dexter noticed Josie's worried frown and nodded, reassuring her that all was well even though he had his doubts. Dexter waved his arm out the truck window, signaling his men to follow him. He drove along an access road that led to the south pasture.

Dexter hoped Dusty returned soon because keeping an eye on Josie and her family was going to be hell on his heart.

SEVERAL HOURS LATER, Dexter and his men arrived with the herd. Josie and her son waited near the entrance to the pasture. Matt stood in his grandfather's truck bed, waving wildly. Dexter lifted a gloved hand in greeting, amused by the kid's enthusiasm.

He questioned whether the boy was happy living in California as Josie insisted. When Dexter had been Matt's age, he and Dusty had spent their days outside, traipsing after their older brothers or running off on their own. They'd caused more trouble than a pack of coon dogs. Dexter's playground had been as far as the eye could see. How big was the play area in Matt's apartment complex—if it even had one?

Dexter signaled Paco to lead the cattle through the gate, which Josie had propped open. Dexter rode toward the pickup.

"Hey, Mr. D! We got drinks." Matt held up a Gatorade bottle.

Dexter halted his horse next to the truck. "Thanks, pardner." He guzzled the liquid, aware of Josie's eyes on him. "That hit the spot."

"I'm gonna go watch." Matt slid off the tailgate and ran to the fence.

Left alone with Josie, Dexter looked his fill. Today she wore her hair in a ponytail pulled through the back of a baseball cap. Standard jeans and bright blue T-shirt. He nodded to the cap. "Dodgers fan?"

"A friend of mine took Matt and me to a game this past spring."

Friend. Male or female? Forcing his thoughts from Josie's personal life, he asked, "How many head of cattle did you say your father had?"

"Fifty at last count."

"We brought in forty-one. There were two carcasses in a gully. The cougar might have gotten those."

She shook her head, her ponytail swishing across her shoulders. "Dad'll have a fit."

"Might be best if he sells off the herd and starts over once he's feeling better."

"He's not a quitter." Josie's brown eyes darkened as they wandered over Dexter's frame, stalling on his thighs before dropping to his boots. What he wouldn't have given for her to look at him like that in high school.

Grateful the saddle horn hid his reaction to her once-over, Dexter backed up his horse, needing the extra space to cool off his body.

"Mom's cooking up a mountain of barbecue. She'd like you and your men to join us for a picnic in the backyard when you're finished here."

Considering how Hank felt about the Codys, Dexter hesitated. "That's nice of your mother but I'd hate to upset your father by—"

"Please stay and eat with us."

A tiny rush of air escaped with her words, drawing his attention to her pink lips. He caved in without a fight. "We should be done in an hour," he said.

"Good." She lifted a cooler from the truck bed and set it on the ground, then called for Matt.

"Aw, Mom. Do we gotta go?" The kid had perfected the hangdog expression.

"Matt can stay. I'll keep an eye on him."

Josie nibbled her lower lip. "He's never ridden on a horse and—" she motioned to the gelding Dexter sat upon "—that's a pretty big horse."

"I won't let anything happen to him, Josie."

Several seconds passed. "Okay. He can stay."

Dexter clicked his tongue and guided the horse over to Matt, determined to keep his attention on the boy and not Josie driving away. He slid off the horse and knelt on one knee in front of Matt. Eye-to-eye he said, "I need your promise that you'll do as I say and keep away from the cattle."

"I promise." Matt flashed his dimple, reminding Dexter of Dusty's mischievous streak. Then the boy flung his arms around Dexter's neck. "Thanks, Mr. D."

Startled by the boy's affection, Dexter wasn't prepared for the warmth that spread through his chest. For a fraction of a second he forgot that Matt was Dusty's child.

"Here's the deal, kid." He walked Matt over to the pasture gate and made him sit on the ground. "Don't budge from this spot. If you follow that rule, you can ride back to your grandpa's house on my horse."

Matt's eyes rounded. "I'm gonna stay right here."

"A real cowboy always keeps his word."

"I wanna be a real cowboy, so I'm not gonna move."

Dexter tipped his hat in salute, then joined his men. He assigned Ricky the job of checking the fence line for breaks or weak spots. Paco backed the water tanker into the pasture, then drove off to fill the stock tanks.

"That heifer there—" Slim pointed to a skinny female "—has pinkeye."

"Damn."

"There's a can of antiseptic spray in the truck," Slim said.

"Better use it on all the cattle." Pinkeye spread like wildfire among cattle and had to be treated daily. Between working with the mustang and caring for Lazy S cattle, Dexter risked spending his entire day at the Lazy S Ranch. Bad idea. It wasn't that he wouldn't enjoy getting to know his nephew better—the boy was a cute buckaroo. Josie was Dexter's big worry—she'd insist on helping out and her help in the barn was the last thing he needed. He hadn't forgotten her sweet scent or watching the swish-sway of her fanny as she pushed the wheelbarrow between the stalls. Shoot, all he'd been able to think about the past twenty-four hours was kissing her.

There can never be anything between you and Josie.

The sooner he got that into his thick skull the better. He had to quit fantasizing about her. Whatever feelings he'd had for Josie in the past had best remain in the past. And he was better off not thinking about the future. Which left only one option—deal with one day at a time.

Dexter helped Slim administer the eye spray and within an hour Ricky and Paco had loaded the horses into the trailer and the group left.

"Ready?" Dexter asked Matt when he walked his horse over to the boy. The kid hadn't budged from his spot.

"He's really big," Matt said, eyeing the horse.

Dexter laid a hand on the boy's shoulder. "Blue's big, but he's gentle." He lifted Matt into the saddle, then climbed up behind him. "Relax and lean against me." Matt obeyed, and Dexter coaxed Blue into a steady trot.

"Sure is bum…bum…py." Matt bounced in the saddle.

"I'm really proud of you," Dexter said, tightening his arm around the boy's waist.

"You are?"

"Yep. You kept your word today."

"That's 'cause I wanna be a real cowboy, like you."

Dexter felt a little tug inside his chest. "What do you like to do on weekends?" He assumed his nephew spent Monday through Friday with a babysitter or in a day care since Josie worked.

"We go to the beach and collect shells. I found a starfish with three legs."

"Do you swim in the ocean?"

"Sometimes, but the water's cold." He glanced up at Dexter. "But horses are better than stupid starfish. I'm gonna tell Brady I rode a horse."

"Who's Brady?"

"He's my bestest friend. Brady doesn't got a dad, either. His dad died."

"Then it's a good thing you're his friend."

"I can make him laugh when he's sad." They rode in silence before Matt spoke again. "Mr. D?"

"What?"

"What if my dad's dead?"

"Why would you think that?"

Tiny shoulders lifted in a shrug. "'Cause I never saw him."

"Your dad's alive, Matt. And you'll see him real soon."

"I wanna tell my dad I rode a horse."

When they arrived in the ranch yard, Paco, Ricky and Slim were jawing by the corral while Josie and her parents waited on the porch. "Sit up real straight," Dexter said. "Your grandpa's watching."

Dexter stopped the horse at the corral, dismounted, then helped Matt. Once the boy's feet hit the ground, he dashed for the house. Slim removed the saddle from Blue and let him loose in the corral with the other horses.

"Grandpa! Mr. D said I'm a real cowboy! And I rode a horse!" Matt tripped and sprawled in the dirt, but bounced up and kept running.

Dexter motioned for the men to follow him. Josie smiled as he drew near, her eyes flashing a silent message of thanks. Dexter introduced the men by name to Josie and her parents.

"My butt's sore." Matt rubbed his hindquarters and everyone laughed.

"We've set the picnic table in the backyard." Josie's mother pointed to the side of the house. "Use the gate."

The men shuffled off and Josie followed her mother inside, Matt trailing behind, leaving Dexter alone with Hank.

"Josie says I'm down to forty-one head."

"Cougar got two."

The rancher shrank before Dexter's eyes.

"I'll warn Jesse to be on the lookout for your brand. If he finds any strays, he'll bring them back." Dexter waited for a cutting remark about his family, but the old man held his tongue.

"You still want to bring that mustang out here?" Hank asked.

Dexter didn't have much choice. If he voiced his reservations, Josie's father would insist on paying Dexter and his men. "That's the plan." Dexter would work with the horse a few more days before making a final decision on relocating him to the Lazy S.

"Then we'll call it even after today." This time Hank offered his hand first. "Best head out back or Phyllis'll squawk at us."

"Mr. Charles," Dexter called when Josie's father turned away.

"Might as well call me Hank now that we've done business together."

"Hank. Pinkeye is spreading through the herd. We sprayed their eyes today, but Bill Chester should take a look at each cow."

"Can't afford a vet."

"Vet call's free. Dr. Bill owes me a few favors." Another lie. How long before he got tangled in the web of lies he kept spouting just to save an old man's pride?

"I'll pay for the medicine." Hank retreated inside the house, and since Dexter didn't receive an invitation to follow, he used the side gate to enter the backyard.

Two picnic tables had been pushed together and draped with a red-checkered cloth. Bowls filled with barbecue pork, potato salad, coleslaw, rolls and a peach cobbler sat in the center of the table.

"Sure does look good, ma'am," Slim said, holding his hat in front of him.

Phyllis placed a pitcher of lemonade on the table. "There's a utility sink on the back porch you men can wash up at."

Dexter waited in line at the sink, then he and his men stood next to the picnic table until Josie and her mother picked their seats.

"I've gotta real bad sweet tooth, ma'am." Ricky grinned. "Mind if I start with dessert?"

"As soon as you say grace you can eat anything you want, young man."

Ricky's jaw dropped, then he fidgeted in his seat. Slim chuckled beneath his breath.

"No need for fancy words." Phyllis spread a napkin in her lap. "A simple thank-you to God will suffice."

"Ah…" Ricky cleared his throat. "Thank you, God, for this great food and Mrs. Charles's peach cobbler."

Amens echoed, then Josie's mother passed the cobbler to Ricky and the rest of the food worked its way around the table with lightning speed.

Josie watched in amazement at how her and her mother's hard work in the kitchen was gobbled up in no time flat. Her appetite, on the other hand, had vanished when she'd caught Dexter watching her. Each time she attempted to make eye contact, he shifted his attention to Matt or the food on his plate.

She wondered how long Dexter would snub the attraction between them. When he continued ignoring her, Josie worried that she'd imagined his interest in her earlier when she and Matt had delivered the Gatorade to the men. Shoot. Maybe she'd read all Dexter's signals wrong. It wasn't as if she had lots of experience with men.

Josie hadn't had a boyfriend since Steve, a court reporter she'd dated after Matt had turned two. The relationship lasted six months before Steve had called it quits. He hadn't been ready for fatherhood and Matt had scared him off.

Ignoring the jittery feeling in her stomach, Josie listened to Slim's stories from his days as a rodeo clown—even her father laughed at a few of the ranch hand's tales. By the time the meal ended the tension between Dexter and her father had eased. The fact a Charles had broken bread with a Cody gave Josie hope that when the time came to reveal the identity of Matt's father, her parents wouldn't blow a gasket.

"Thank you, ma'am, for the meal." Ricky patted his stomach. "Best cobbler I've ever tasted."

"It's been a while since I cooked for cowboys. Next time I'll remember to double the servings." Josie's mother began collecting the empty bowls.

"How's about a little music while our food settles?" Slim removed a harmonica from his pocket.

"What's that?" Matt asked.

"A tin sandwich." Slim pressed his mouth to the piece and heavenly sounds filled the air.

"Always wanted to learn how to play one of those things," Josie's father said. "You know 'The Old Chisholm Trail'?"

"Well, now, let's see if I remember...." Slim played and Ricky sang along, slapping his hand against his thigh. Then Josie's parents joined in at the chorus.

As soon as the song ended, Dexter stood. "Mrs. Charles, I'd like to thank you for your hospitality, but we'd best head home."

Dexter shook Josie's father's hand, tipped his hat to her mother and patted Matt on the back. "I'll see you soon for another riding lesson."

Where's my goodbye?

While the ranch hands showered Mrs. Charles with more compliments on the meal, Dexter sneaked out the side gate. Josie followed.

"Dex, wait." She trotted to catch up to him. "Is everything all right?"

"What? Um, yeah, everything's fine." He stopped at his truck. "I forgot to mention Dusty called this morning." His neutral expression gave no clue if the call had been good or bad.

"Oh?"

"He's not sure when he'll leave Canada, but he asked that I look after you and Matt."

Dexter had gone to all the trouble to move Lazy S cattle out of an obligation to his brother and not because…because…*of me.* "Matt and I don't need looking after. We've managed fine on our own."

Her comment drew a grimace from Dexter. He cleared his throat. "One of the heifers has a bad case of pinkeye. Bill Chester will be out tomorrow to examine the cow."

"Are you coming with him?" She winced at the breathless note in her voice, but forgot her embarrassment the moment Dexter's blue-eyed stare latched onto her mouth. Her lips tingled from the intensity of his stare.

"I hadn't planned to. I've got chores to catch up on and a stallion to work with."

The cold note in Dexter's voice signaled his intention to put some distance between them. Why was she surprised? Hadn't he been the one to step back from their friendship in high school? What did it matter if she and Dexter never renewed their friendship—once Dusty returned and they informed their parents about Matt, all hell would break loose between the families. The Codys were a fiercely loyal clan.

No matter how she and Dexter felt about each other, he'd never take her side.

Chapter Six

"You sure you wanna go in there with him?" Big Ben asked Dexter as the men stood outside the round pen.

"Yep." Earlier in the morning Dexter had phoned Josie to remind her he wouldn't be accompanying the vet to check on her father's cows, because he'd intended to work with the mustang. In reality he'd spouted the excuse to avoid Josie altogether. He might not be with her physically, but his mind was having a heck of a time letting go of the woman.

"He needs to be pushed." Dexter referred to the horse. The stallion was the most stubborn animal he'd ever worked with. He would have to do more than *whisper* if he intended to board the mustang at the Lazy S. Masterson claimed he hadn't wanted to name the animal until he was certain he'd keep him. But a horse as magnificent and prideful as this one deserved a title of respect. Dexter decided to call him Zeus—because this stallion had ruled his world before he'd been captured.

Right now Dexter wished he had the power to control his world. If he did, he'd ban Josie from his thoughts. Last night she'd visited his dreams. First, they'd sat together in English class. Next, they'd parked at the drive-in movies. Later they'd danced at the Spotted Horse Saloon. And then they'd kissed… Dexter had woken in a cold sweat.

What was the matter with him? Josie was off-limits. She and Matt belonged with Dusty. Whatever Dexter had felt for her in high school had ended in high school. That he hadn't been brave enough to tell her how he'd felt all those years ago was nobody's fault but his own. Shame settled over his shoulders like a wet horse blanket. No decent man would covet his brother's woman.

And it was only a matter of time before Dusty and Josie agreed that the best road for them to take was the one that led straight to the altar. Dexter had feared if he'd tried to fall asleep again he would continue to dream of Josie, so he'd filled a thermos with coffee and sat with Zeus until sunrise.

"Here." Big Ben held out a nylon web halter with a flat cotton lunge line. Dexter wore a pair of leather work gloves to prevent rope burns because he didn't trust the stallion not to fight him.

Ricky exited the barn. "I got twenty bucks that says the mustang won't let Dexter get close enough to put a halter on him."

"I'll see your twenty and raise you twenty more that the boss gets a halter on Zeus," Big Ben said.

"Is that all my life's worth—forty bucks?" Dexter grinned.

"I want in." Slim joined the group.

"For or against me?" Dexter asked.

"Boss, only a fool would bet against you. Fifty bucks says you get a halter on the horse." Slim spit tobacco at the ground.

Dexter smirked at Ricky. "Care to change your wager?"

"Nope. You're going down," Ricky said.

"We'll see about that." Dexter pulled the brim of his hat to settle it more snugly on his head. "Now everybody quiet and leave me to my whispering."

The men backed up a respectable distance and remained silent. Dexter closed his eyes and took deep breaths, until the tension drained from his body. The problem was when he relaxed, so did his brain and darned if Josie didn't find a way to slip past his defenses.

He could blame his initial attraction to Josie on nostalgic feelings from days gone by. Or that he was horny because he hadn't been with another woman since Shannon. But the truth was…Josie intrigued him more today than she had in high school, which made no sense. She was tied tighter to Dusty now than ever before. He admired Josie for raising a child on her own and not looking to a man to rescue her.

But as much as Dexter respected Josie's independent spirit, he didn't understand or condone her decision not to inform Dusty of her pregnancy. Dusty had already lost four years with his son, and Dexter was determined that he wouldn't get in the way or give Josie a reason to change her mind about allowing Dusty and the Codys to be a part of Matt's life.

Family comes first. Dexter was closer to Dusty than any of his siblings. They were more than brothers—they were twins. Their bond went deeper than most brothers' and, by God, Dexter refused to destroy their relationship because he couldn't control his impulses around Josie.

Zeus neighed, startling Dexter. He opened his eyes to find the mustang had moved closer to the gate. Had the horse sensed Dexter's distress?

"Would you look at that," Ricky whispered. "He made Zeus come to him."

"Quiet or the horse will bolt," Big Ben said.

You may not believe it, Zeus, but this halter is your lifeline. You have to trust humans or you'll be running wild in Heaven not on earth.

The mustang pawed the dirt and snorted. His eyes pleaded for mercy.

No can do, big guy. Dexter opened the gate and stepped inside the pen. The animal's hindquarters bunched, ready for flight.

Nice and easy... One step forward.

The stallion stood his ground, boldly daring Dexter to crowd him.

Trust me, Zeus. Another step forward. Then another. Dexter stopped nose-to-nose with the stallion. *Lower your head.*

Zeus raised his head and snorted, spraying Dexter's shirt.

That's okay. I'm a patient man. Slowly, he lifted the halter.

The stallion backed up, paused, then moved forward, nudging the nylon halter with his nose.

Dexter gently eased the contraption over the horse's head.

"Well, heck," Ricky grumbled.

Zeus's body quivered with tension as Dexter held up the lunge line. The stallion didn't appear interested in the rope, so Dexter clipped it to the harness.

Then all hell broke loose.

Zeus reared, pawing the air. Dexter dropped the rope and stepped back. His right boot heel came down on a chunk of carrot that must have fallen out of one of the hands' pockets. His ankle twisted and Dexter stumbled. Everything happened in a blur. The sound of the gate opening reached Dexter's ears. Just as he crawled to his knees, Zeus's hoof connected with Dexter's butt, sending him back into the dirt. Then someone grabbed his arms and dragged him out of the pen.

"You all right, boss?" Big Ben asked.

Damn, his ass hurt. "Help me up," Dexter said. As soon as he stood pain shot through his right butt cheek.

"Maybe a doctor ought to take a look at your backside." Slim's grin almost split his face in half.

"I guess I'm out fifty bucks," Ricky said. Then he nudged Slim in the arm. "You'll have to wait until payday. I got a date with Karleen Saturday night."

While Slim and Ben harassed Ricky about his date, Dexter hobbled off to lick his wounded pride. Zeus was turning out to be a real pain in the ass—literally.

Riding lessons with Matt would have to be put on hold for a few days—until Dexter could haul himself up on a horse. Considering he was so torn up inside over Josie, the kick in the behind might have been just what he'd needed. By the time his butt cheek healed, he'd have figured out how to erect a wall between him and Josie.

"When's Mr. D gonna let me ride a horse again?" Matt asked Josie as the pickup bumped along a dirt road on her father's ranch. She'd planned a Saturday-afternoon fishing trip in hopes her son would forget Dexter's promise. Fat chance.

"Mr. D's a very busy man, honey." Even though she suspected Dusty's absence added to Dexter's work-load, she couldn't shake the feeling that something was wrong. In all the years she'd known Dexter, he'd never reneged on a pledge. "I'm sure he'll stop by Grandpa's ranch soon."

This past Wednesday Bill Chester had arrived alone to treat her father's herd for pinkeye. Josie had hoped Dexter would change his mind and accompany the veterinarian but he'd been a no-show. Three days had passed since the vet's visit.

Three long days.

"How come Grandpa didn't wanna go fishing?"

"He needs his rest." Her poor father was exhausted—not so much from physical exertion but from worry. He agonized over J.W.'s reaction when he learned that his son had come to the aid of the enemy. Her father insisted Dexter had an ulterior motive, and Josie hadn't been able to deny the charge. She didn't dare confess the real reason Dexter had helped them—Matt was a Cody. She feared the news would upset her father and cause a relapse. Then yesterday morning she'd found her mother studying Matt with a speculative gleam in her eye and Josie figured her mother suspected Matt might be a Cody.

After Josie had broken the news of her pregnancy to her parents she'd told them that the father hadn't wanted to be involved in their lives. Her parents had badgered her with questions but finally dropped the subject when

Josie had remained closemouthed. Once Dusty returned from Canada they'd tell both families, and she'd deal with the fallout then.

"Can you teach me to ride a horse?" Matt asked.

"If Mr. D doesn't come around soon, I will." She'd ridden plenty of horses as a child, but the Codys were experts at handling the animals and she'd rather have her son learn from one of the best.

Dexter…Dexter…Dexter.

Whenever she and Dusty had had a spat, Dexter had always been there for her. He'd offered her his ear, a shoulder and sometimes a Kleenex. And then over Christmas break their senior year he hadn't been there. Josie had never been able to figure out what had happened to change Dexter's feelings toward her. She'd even asked Dusty if something was wrong with his brother but Dusty had blown off her concern and told her not to worry.

"Who's gonna teach me how to fish?"

"I am."

"Girls can't fish."

Josie laughed. "Grandpa showed me how to bait a hook when I was your age."

"Did you fish a lot?"

"Until I was thirteen." Then she'd entered junior high and life revolved around boys.

The road came to a T and instead of veering right and keeping on Lazy S property, Josie took the left fork and drove onto Cody land toward an offshoot of the Shoshone River. The tributary was forty feet wide and fast flowing. She and Dusty had swum there during the summer months when the water warmed enough that it didn't steal your breath.

After parking the truck she said, "Here are the rules."

"Aw, Mom."

"If you don't obey the rules, we go back to the house."

"Okay."

"No wading into the water—" she narrowed her eyes when he opened his mouth to protest "—unless I'm holding your hand. Second rule, no touching the fish hooks in the tackle box. Third rule, no wandering into the woods." The stream wasn't anywhere near where the cougar had been sighted, but she intended to keep her guard up.

"Can you teach me how to use Grandpa's gun?" Matt pointed to the weapon stowed in the locked rack in the truck's rear window.

"That's rule number four. No touching the shotgun." As much as Josie considered herself a big-city girl, she couldn't shake her country roots. Her father had taught her how to load and shoot the gun at an early age. He'd insisted she carry the weapon in case they crossed paths with a wild animal.

"Here." Josie handed Matt the old quilt she'd packed along with the fishing gear. "Spread the blanket near the stream while I fetch the tackle box and poles."

Five minutes later, Josie prepared Matt's hook. "That's a fake fish, Mom." Matt pointed to the lure Josie chose from the tackle box.

"It's called crankbait—it's supposed to resemble a miniature fish. This stream is full of brown trout and they eat little fish." At her son's doubtful expression, Josie smiled. "Wait and see." She checked the tension on the line, then showed Matt how to hold the pole.

Together they cast the line toward a cluster of logs downstream. "Good job. If you feel a tug on the line, grip the pole tight to keep it from flying out of your hands when the trout bites down on the crankbait."

"Okay."

Josie retreated to the quilt and as soon as she settled into a comfortable position, Matt shouted, "Mom!"

Startled, Josie sprang to her feet, her eyes searching the woods for a predator.

"I got a fish!"

"Don't scare me like that." She rushed to Matt's side and helped steady the pole. "Easy now."

"The fish is gonna break it."

"The pole's fine," she assured. "Let the fish fight for a minute." Inch by inch they reeled the line in until the fish emerged from the stream. "Congratulations, Matt. It's a brown trout." She reached into her back pocket for a glove and slipped it on her right hand. Once she had a solid grasp on the fish, she removed the hook.

"Gross." Matt made an ugly face.

"Fill the bucket with water from the stream."

"You said not to go in the water."

Good grief. "Stay right at the edge and dip the bucket into the stream. Be careful you don't slip."

Matt did as instructed, then asked, "Why'd you put the fish in there?" He dropped to his knees and peered inside the bucket.

"If we catch bigger fish we'll throw the smaller ones back."

"Are we gonna eat the fish?" Matt scrunched his face in distaste.

Josie chuckled. "Trust me. You'll like Grandma's recipe for grilled fish." Josie's mouth watered thinking about supper. "Ready to try again?" she asked.

"Yeah, but I wanna bait the hook."

Her son's stubborn streak reminded her more of Dexter than Dusty. Handing the crankbait to her son, she said, "Be careful you don't poke your finger." When he managed to bait the hook without stabbing himself, she breathed a sigh of relief and moved aside so he could cast the line. After a few attempts, he landed the bobber in the middle of the stream.

"Looks like you two are having fun."

Josie spun, her heartbeat doubling at the sight of Dexter. No other man had ever thrown her off balance the way he did. Today he wore faded jeans with a big ol' rodeo buckle, scruffy boots, a tight black T-shirt that emphasized his muscular arms and chest, which drew her attention to the faded patch of denim that concealed his zipper. Add a five o' clock shadow at three in the afternoon and the cowboy was flat-out *hot*.

"What are you doing here?" Her question sounded breathless to her own ears, and she cursed herself for acting like a jittery teenager. No wonder she hadn't heard him approach—he'd ridden Sugar, one of her father's horses.

"I stopped—"

"Hey, Mr. D, I got another fish." Matt struggled to hold the pole.

Dexter moved forward with a pronounced limp and helped Matt reel in his second brown trout. "Looks like you're quite the fisherman, squirt." Dexter removed the hook and placed the fish into the bucket.

"Mom's teaching me to fish 'cause you didn't show me how to ride a horse again."

Josie winced at her son's bluntness.

"I'm sorry about that, Matt." Dexter ruffled the blond head. "I had an accident."

"What happened?" Josie nodded to his leg.

"The mustang I've been working with got a little feisty and kicked me."

Good Lord, Dexter could have been seriously injured. "Are you all right?"

He rubbed his backside. "Bruised pride." He helped Matt bait the hook, then cast the line before handing the pole over. "I stopped by your parents' house. Your dad said you'd gone fishing. Figured this is where I'd find you." He stared into space, and Josie wondered if he was recalling the afternoons she'd spent with him and Dusty swimming and fishing.

Dexter had hung around her and Dusty a lot—and then he'd quit talking to her. Josie hadn't thought anything unusual about Dexter accompanying her and Dusty on outings. Most twins were close. She studied Dexter—his blue eyes appeared greener today. "Can I ask you something?"

"Sure."

"Why did you tag along with Dusty and me all the time?"

The quiet hitch in his breath was the only indication the question surprised him.

"Do you want the truth or something made up?" he asked.

"The truth."

"I was afraid Dusty might make a move on you."
What?

Dexter glanced at Matt, then lowered his voice. "Dusty wanted to have sex with you. He told me."

Josie clasped her hands against her cheeks and moaned. "Did Dusty tell you everything that happened between us?" She'd been a virgin until Dusty and frankly the few times they'd fumbled around with sex hadn't been anything to brag about.

Dexter grinned. "He said you weren't very good at it."

She gasped. "Well, neither was he." Waving a hand in front of her face, she insisted, "I only did it with him because I was afraid of losing him to some other girl." No wonder most people refused to revisit their adolescent years and reminisce over the foolish mistakes they'd made.

"I had a crush on you in high school, Josie. But you only had eyes for Dusty." His gaze softened on her face. "I followed you and Dusty around because I wanted to be with you and I couldn't stand the thought of you being alone with my brother."

Oh, my. She'd asked for the truth and she'd gotten it. She sucked in a deep breath to calm her thumping heart. *What-ifs* stampeded through her mind—one-second bleeps of images from the past. Why hadn't Dexter declared his interest in her back then?

Because family comes first with the Codys, and Dexter would never try to take what belonged to his brother.

But had she known Dexter's feelings she might have gone out with him instead of Dusty.

No, you wouldn't have. You liked being part of the limelight that followed Dusty wherever he went.

"I have a confession to make," she said. "I liked you better than Dusty."

His eyes widened. "Then why—"

She raised a hand. "It doesn't make sense, I know, but Dusty was crazy and wild and what teenage girl didn't want to be with him?" She picked at an imaginary spec of lint on her jeans. "When we were together all he talked about was rodeo and how good he was. We never had a serious conversation about the future and he never asked what plans I had after high school." She smiled. "But you did, remember?"

"We were all crazy back then," he said.

"Is that why you gave me the cold shoulder our senior year—because you didn't want me to date Dusty?"

"Yeah. I hated that you two were sleeping together. I figured keeping my distance was the only way me and Dusty wouldn't come to blows."

Josie's throat swelled with emotion. She'd always wondered what she'd done to drive Dexter away. Learning the reason hardly made her feel better.

"Hey, Mom. I got another one!"

Matt's shout ended her conversation with Dexter. A half hour later with a total of five fish in the bucket, Josie announced it was time to head home.

"If it's okay with your mom, Matt, I thought you might like to ride Sugar with me to your grandpa's house."

"Can I, Mom?"

"Are you sure?" She motioned to Dexter's bum leg.

"I'm fine."

"You listen to Mr. D and do what he says." She brushed the hair from her son's eyes.

Matt shrugged off her touch. Okay she got the message—*don't treat me like a baby.* "See you at the house." She hopped into the truck and drove off. When she glanced in the rearview mirror the big buckaroo was setting the little buckaroo in the saddle.

A pain pierced Josie's heart. They looked so right together. Why couldn't Dexter have been Matt's father?

"HANG ON, MATT." DEXTER said as he eased into the saddle behind the boy.

"How come you always call me Matt?"

"Don't your friends call you Matt?"

"Nope. They call me Mattie."

"You want me to call you Mattie?"

"I guess you can call me Matt." The boy's skinny chest puffed up.

"First rule—"

"Oh, man. Mom always gots rules, too."

"Rules are good. They keep us out of trouble. Now, rule number one—never, ever scare a horse. Don't run, scream or make any sudden movements around them."

"How come?"

"If a horse becomes frightened they might step on your foot or kick you." He reached past the boy and patted the mare's neck. "You want to be gentle with a horse. If you respect Sugar and treat her well, she'll return the favor."

"Can I pet her?"

Dexter tightened his hold around Matt's waist and the boy leaned forward to stroke the horse's mane.

"When we get back to the barn I'll show you how to groom Sugar."

"What's a groom?"

"Grooming is rule number two. Always keep your horse fed, watered and clean." Dexter reached inside the saddlebag. "This—" he held up a child's riding helmet "—is rule number three."

"I gotta wear a helmet."

"Yep." Dexter adjusted the chin strap and made sure it was securely fastened. He'd purchased the helmet at Markton Feed and Grain when he'd gone into town yesterday. He'd felt guilty that he'd allowed his confused feelings for Josie, not his injury, to keep him from giving Matt a riding lesson.

"Hold the reins loosely and don't tug on them. Sugar knows the way home."

"Mr. D?"

"What?"

"Are horses as smart as people?"

Dexter relaxed, grateful Matt's questions offered a reprieve from his obsession with Josie.

Chapter Seven

Tuesday morning Dexter drove his rig and horse trailer to the Lazy S and found Hank Charles waiting by the barn. Dexter got out of the truck and lifted a hand in greeting, then glanced at the house expecting Josie to appear.

"She went into town to run errands," Hank said as he walked across the gravel drive. He nodded to the trailer. "You decide to bring the mustang out here after all?"

"The stallion's calmed down enough that I don't believe he'll try to break free." After the kick in the backside Dexter had worked long hours with the horse and the lunge line. Hank stood aside when Dexter opened the trailer doors.

"Beautiful piece of horseflesh. Who'd you say he belongs to?" Hank walked ahead and opened the corral gate.

"Bud Masterson. He owns a ranch in Montana. Rescued Zeus from a trip to the glue factory."

"Zeus?"

"Had to call him something other than *horse*." Dexter led the mustang into the corral, removed the rope and bridle, then patted the animal's neck—an act the stallion had consented to only this morning before being coaxed into the trailer.

Dexter filled the water trough and added grain to the feed bins attached to the metal rails. "You picked a great spot for this corral." He propped a boot on the lower rung next to Hank. Located on the east side of the barn, the enclosed area received morning sun and afternoon shade provided by the barn and a dense cluster of cottonwood trees.

"Years ago Walter Pennyton owned the Lazy S. Phyllis and I had just married when I hired on to work his cattle. She talked Pennyton into planting the seedlings."

"The trees must be close to seventy feet tall," Dexter said. The cottonwoods towered over the barn. Tree talk depleted, Dexter changed the subject. "Bob Simms phoned my father and said one of his hands shot the cougar that's been stalking the area."

"If Simms had stuck with cattle instead of trading them in for sheep we wouldn't have cougar problems in the area."

That wasn't really true, but Dexter refrained from commenting. He believed a man ought to be able to do what he pleased with his property. He'd grown up around cattle and horses and didn't care for the fuzzy lambs, but Simms had been a good neighbor through the years and Dexter's mother called Simms's wife, Leonna, a good friend.

"How are the cows doing?" Dexter asked.

"Vet attached insecticide tags to their ears to keep the flies away from their eyes."

Dexter knew that—the bill for the service sat on the dresser in his bedroom.

"Hardly seems a fair trade for boarding your mustang, especially when you're supplying the feed for my herd."

"As soon as Dr. Bill gives the all clear to your cattle, we'll herd them back to the valley."

Hank shook his head. "Still can't figure out what angle you're playing."

"What you mean?"

"You're either helping me because J.W.'s got something up his sleeve or you're after my little girl."

Startled by Hank's accusation, Dexter was at a loss for words.

"I'm old and my heart's ticking on borrowed time, but I'm not blind. I've seen the way your eyes follow Josie."

Had he been that obvious? Face heating, Dexter said, "Josie and I were good friends in high school."

"Back then she only had time for your brother." Hank scoffed. "Dusty was the wild one. Far as I remember you were the quiet, polite twin."

"I'll agree with you that I wasn't as flamboyant as my brother, but I'm positive my mother would refute your compliment on my good manners."

"Haven't seen Dusty around town in months. What's that brother of yours been up to?"

Why did Dexter get the feeling Hank was fishing for information about his twin? Did the old man suspect Dusty of being Matt's father? "He's training horses on a movie set up in Canada."

"Don't surprise me none. That boy always did like the limelight."

"Mind me asking what you've got against us Codys?"

Hank's eyes narrowed to a slit. "That's between me and J.W."

"If I ask my father will he tell me to mind my own business, too?"

"Most likely he'll lie to you."

Dexter's hackles rose. "You sound pretty sure of that."

"You interested in the truth?"

"Yes, sir." Dexter would love to learn what had caused the animosity between the two men.

"C'mon. I'll show you why your father hates my guts."

Dexter shortened his steps to match the older man's slower pace. When they entered the house, Hank said, "Phyllis is out in the garden." He opened a door in the kitchen and flipped on a light switch, then descended the steps into the cellar.

Musty, damp air filled Dexter's nostrils. The concrete walls had been sealed, as had the floor, but no drywall had been hung or carpet installed. A washer and dryer sat in one corner along with an aluminum table for folding clothes. An ironing board stood propped against the wall and an iron sat alongside an old radio on the counter next to the utility sink. The rest of the space was crowded with old furniture covered in plastic and cardboard boxes stacked against two of the walls. Hank opened the door to the root cellar and tugged the string attached to a naked lightbulb in the ceiling.

The twelve-by-twelve room housed floor-to-ceiling shelves that had at one time held dozens of canning jars. Now the shelves were crammed with rodeo trophies.

"J.W. couldn't keep his arse on a horse if he was tied down to one." Hank's mouth tilted in a smile.

Dexter's thoughts flew back in time to the day he'd helped haul several boxes of books up to the attic in the old house. He'd come across his father's trophies—second and third place mostly. When Dexter asked about the awards his father had changed the subject. "Dad never talks about his rodeo days."

"Because he's a sore loser." Hank pointed to a trophy with Riverside High etched into the tarnished nameplate. "J.W. and I had a fearsome rivalry for years." He shrugged. "Don't know if I was dumb lucky or if pure determination to beat the rich kid kept me from being thrown."

Dexter recognized a state trophy. "Runner-up National Finals Rodeo. That's pretty impressive."

"Your father was mad as a peeled rattler when he didn't make the qualifying round that year." Hank returned the trophy to the shelf. "I always believed J.W. was disappointed Phyllis couldn't have any more babies after Josie."

"Why do you say that?"

"I reckon he was counting on the next generation of Codys to put the Charles kids in their place. J.W.'s pushed you boys from a young age to be the best in rodeo."

Pushed was a strong word. However, Dexter couldn't remember a time when his father ever suggested Dexter try a different sport. As a matter of fact, the Cody wealth gave him and his siblings every advantage when it came to rodeo. They had the best horses, best equipment, best instructors, best *everything*.

"How come Josie never got involved in rodeo?" Dexter asked. The subject had somehow never come up between him and Josie in school.

"I wanted Josie to compete in barrel racing but my daughter never took to horses or ranch life the way I'd hoped."

Josie hadn't been a typical ranch kid. Sure, she'd worn jeans to school but with a frilly top or ruffled blouse—unlike the other girls who'd preferred Western blouses. And Josie had styled her hair—curls one day, straight the next, but rarely in the traditional country-girl ponytail.

When he thought back to high school and all the conversations he and Josie had shared about the future, she'd been determined not to hang around Markton any longer than she'd had to. She'd been positive the world held more for her than cowboys and horses. Was there a chance Josie might learn to appreciate Markton now that she'd lived on both sides of the mountain—so to speak?

"I can understand being upset over coming in second all the time but that was years ago." Dexter studied Hank. "My father doesn't cling to his past. I suspect there's another reason fueling the grudge match between you two."

"Better ask J.W. He'll want you to hear his side of the story first."

Dexter suspected whatever had transpired between Hank and J.W. had played a role in Josie's decision to keep Matt a secret from her family and the Codys. The sound of a truck horn ended the question-answer session. Hank turned out the light. "Bet that's Josie and Matt."

Hank headed outside and Dexter followed, stumbling to a halt when he saw Josie in the front seat of Mark Hansen's truck. Never mind that Matt sat between the pair—what was Josie doing with the bull rider?

Jealousy grabbed hold of Dexter and yanked hard. He had nothing against Hansen. The man was a decent bull rider. As a matter of fact the cowboy was giving Jesse a run for his money on the bull-riding circuit. It was anyone's guess which man would go all the way to the NFR.

"Dexter," Hansen hollered when he got out of the truck. He tipped his hat. "Mr. Charles."

"Howdy, Mark," Hank greeted, then asked, "Where's my truck?"

"Ran out of gas a few miles up the road." Josie smiled at Hansen—too sweetly in Dexter's opinion. "Lucky for me Mark happened by and offered Matt and me a lift home."

Yeah, real lucky.

Clutching an object in his hands, Matt raced across the drive and up the porch steps.

"Whatcha got there?" Dexter asked.

"Mr. Hansen gave this to me." The boy held up a small pocketknife. "He said I can carve stuff from wood."

What had Hansen been thinking, giving a boy Matt's age something he could poke his eye out with?

"I told Mr. Hansen you were teaching me to ride a horse and he said you could show me how to use the knife, too." Unlike his mother, Matt hadn't fallen under the bull rider's spell.

"Sure, I can teach you how to use the knife."

"If you've got a full gas can lying around I'll run Josie back out to your truck and fill the tank," Hansen said.

Over my dead body. Dexter descended the porch steps. "I'll take care of it." He always carried a full gas can in the back of his truck for emergencies.

"I'm gonna show Grandma my knife." Matt disappeared into the house.

"It's no trouble driving Josie down the highway," Hansen insisted.

"I'm heading in that direction." Ignoring Hank's quiet chuckle, Dexter walked over to his rig and unhitched the horse trailer. "Coming, Josie?" He hopped in the truck and gunned the engine, then switched the air conditioner to high, hoping the blast of cold air would cool his temper. He hated acting like a jealous teenager. He had no claim on Josie, even though a part of him wished he had.

He slid on his sunglasses and peered out the windshield. Josie went up on tiptoe and hugged Hansen, then stood there and waved goodbye as the man drove off. Dexter gripped the steering wheel until the skin over his knuckles threatened to split. "What was that all about?" he asked when she joined him in the truck. He shifted into gear and followed Hansen's dust cloud to the main road.

"What was *what* about?"

"Since when did you and Hansen hook up?"

"We haven't hooked up."

Keep your mouth shut. "Do you always hug strangers?"

"We all went to the same school, Dex. We're hardly strangers."

He glanced across the seat, then wished he'd kept his eyes on the road. Josie's windblown hair made her look as if she'd crawled out of bed after a long night of lovemaking. Her brown eyes glittered with anger, but he suspected they'd shine just as bright with passion.

"Dexter Cody…"

"What?" He honked a *thanks* when Hansen reached the county road and turned in the opposite direction.

"You're jealous," Josie said.

"I'm not…*jealous*." He changed the subject. "Matt shouldn't be playing with a pocketknife."

"Oh, for goodness' sake. I bet you got your first knife at his age."

"That's irrelevant. Matt's a city kid and doesn't have the same experience country kids have."

"What do you mean?" she asked.

"You probably tell Matt not to talk to strangers."

"Of course I do. Perverts who prey on kids are everywhere these days."

"And kids raised around Markton are taught to stop and help a stranger in need." Dexter exhaled loudly. "Matt lives in a different world than kids around here."

Snort. "Did my father do something to put you in this grumpy mood?"

Feeling his control slip, he said, "You want to know why I'm upset?"

"Upset? You're acting like a bear with a splinter in his paw."

Enough was enough. Dexter swung the truck onto the shoulder of the road, hit the brakes, shifted into Park and released his seat belt. "This is why I'm upset." He leaned across the seat, grasped Josie's face and kissed the sass out of her.

Good Lord! Stunned by the feel of Dexter's mouth moving against hers, Josie didn't immediately respond to his kiss.

Dexter paused, his lips brushing hers when he spoke. "Want me to stop?"

"No." The word slipped from her mouth on a sigh. Josie closed her eyes and gave herself over to the tingles racing through her limbs. Several gentle, slow brushes of his mouth against hers, then his tongue delved inside. Light-headed, she curled a hand around his neck and slid her fingers into his hair, then melted into a puddle of heat.

While his tongue explored, his hand glided down her neck, fingers brushing aside the collar of her blouse before continuing south until he found her breast.

The subtle scent of Dexter's maleness combined with his aftershave made her woozy. Never had a man kissed her with such obsession—as if she were his world. His universe. His reason for being.

Josie had had two lovers in her lifetime. Her job and raising Matt left little room for a relationship. Most men her age refused to become involved with a woman who already had a child.

Dexter's not most men.

Before passion overruled common sense Josie's brain insisted this was just a kiss.…

But then Dexter's hand unsnapped her seat belt, and she launched herself against him, kissing him like a love-starved harlot. She straddled his thigh, pressed her breasts against his chest and moaned into his mouth.

The sounds of heavy breathing filled the truck cab. She fumbled with the buttons on his shirt, managing to free two from their holes when a vehicle whizzed past and laid on the horn.

Startled, she bolted across the seat and leaned against the passenger door.

Dexter got out of the truck, then stumble-walked several feet along the shoulder of the road before stopping to stare into the distance.

While Josie adjusted her clothing, she took shallow breaths, hoping to slow her erratic heartbeat. *Wow.* With one kiss Dexter had blown her world to smithereens. She tapped her fingertips against her swollen lips and closed her eyes.

Her sexual attraction to Dexter frightened her. Becoming intimately involved with her son's uncle was *so* not a good idea. She liked Dexter a lot—okay, more than a lot. She admired his generosity in helping her father and appreciated the way he'd taken Matt under his wing. There wasn't much not to like about the man.

Until both families were told the truth—that Dusty was Matt's father—she'd better not complicate the situation by becoming involved with Dexter. She studied his lone figure alongside the road. Did he regret kissing her? She left the truck and approached him. "Is everything okay?"

He spun. "I don't know. You tell me, Josie."

Hoping to erase the frown across his brow she said, "It was just a kiss."

The frown deepened. "You sure about that?"

No. She crushed a pebble beneath her boot heel while she considered his question.

"Hell." He paced in front of her. "My brother is Matt's father."

"Your point being…?"

He motioned to her, then himself. "We can't do this. It's wrong."

Her heart sighed. Why did Dexter have to be such a good guy? The kind of man who put others before himself? Who took the high road? *You wouldn't be so enamored with him if he wasn't.* Dexter was exactly the kind of man Josie yearned for.

His blue eyes pinned her. "I can't…won't come between my brother and his son."

"Our relationship has nothing to do with Matt and Dusty."

"You and Dusty haven't had time to discuss the future."

"What future?" Other than sharing a child, Josie and Dusty had no relationship.

The lines around Dexter's mouth relaxed. "Might be best if you told me where you stand with Dusty."

"We're not in love with one another. What I felt for your brother years ago was a teenage crush."

"Obviously those feelings stuck around or Matt wouldn't be here."

"Do you want to hear what happened between me and Dusty? It's not as exciting as you're making it out to be."

Dexter averted his eyes, and Josie imagined that he struggled with wanting yet not wanting to know the intimate details of Matt's conception. If Dexter chose not to hear her out that meant he wanted to forget their kiss. Josie, on the other hand, did not want to forget the kiss.

"I'm listening," he said.

Her knees wobbled with relief. "I had just begun my first court-reporting job when the elevator doors in the Smith-Davidson Building in downtown L.A. opened and there stood your brother." She rushed on before Dexter changed his mind about listening. "Dusty said he was in town on business. He insisted on taking me out to dinner to celebrate my new job. I offered for him to stay at my apartment instead of a hotel, because my roommate was out of town visiting her parents." Now that four years had passed she could look back on that time with an unprejudiced eye.

"We never meant for anything to happen. But we began talking about the past and dating in high school, and then we shared a bottle of wine, and, well, it was one of those for-old-times'-sake things. I hadn't been involved with anyone in a long time and I guess I was lonely."

"You two didn't take precautions?"

"We did. But the condoms in the medicine cabinet had expired." She shrugged. "The next morning I woke up and Dusty was gone."

"I'm sorry he hurt you, Josie."

"Dusty didn't hurt me. I was grateful in a way." She rushed to explain. "After I left Markton I'd always believed there was a part of me that would love Dusty forever. But that night proved I had moved on."

"And then you found out you were pregnant with Matt."

"Yes. At first, I worried that carrying Dusty's child might reignite my feelings for him." She smiled. "But that wasn't the case."

Regardless of Josie's lack of feelings for Dusty, Dexter would stand by his brother. His twin had a say in what happened with Josie and Matt and no matter how Josie tempted Dexter—and, man, did she tempt—he had no business becoming involved with his nephew's mother. "We'd better gas up your truck."

If they didn't get going he'd kiss her again. And one kiss would lead to another and then another and eventually trouble bigger than the state of Wyoming.

Chapter Eight

Saturday morning Dexter brushed Digger's coat until sweat beaded his brow. He'd risen at dawn to check on the horses and give instructions to the hands before he left the ranch for the day. Earlier in the week he'd promised Josie and Matt he'd take them to the National Little Britches Rodeo at the Wilson County Fairgrounds in Powell, a small town northwest of Markton.

Nothing he did anymore made sense. He was determined to keep his distance from Josie, yet at the same time he couldn't get close enough to her. He shouldn't have suggested the rodeo, but he figured he wouldn't be spending time alone with Josie and Matt once Dusty returned. Dexter wanted a few memories of his own to tuck away in his heart before he was forced to give Dusty, Josie and Matt a wide berth while they worked through their plans for the future.

After the roadside kiss they'd shared this past Tuesday, spending a minute, much less a day, with Josie probably wasn't a smart move on Dexter's part. Matt's presence might convince Dexter to keep his hands to himself but the little tyke couldn't prevent Dexter from fantasizing about the boy's mother and the feelings she stirred in him.

The kiss should never have happened—no matter how attractive he found Josie. No matter that he enjoyed her company. No matter that he genuinely liked her. No matter…nothing. Josie was off-limits. Period.

He blamed his weakness for her on the fact that his breakup with Shannon had left him gutted and lonely. He'd truly loved Shannon and had been looking forward to settling down with her and starting a family—Josie was a sad reminder of that lost dream. She and Matt were Dusty's instant family—not his.

Dexter yearned to believe that Josie had spoken the truth—the torch she'd once carried for his brother had burned out. But that was years ago. Life threw curveballs, forcing people to adjust. Dusty and Josie deserved a chance to rekindle their feelings for one another—they owed it to themselves and to Matt to try and be a family. Dusty might not be in love with Josie but he was bound to hold affectionate feelings for her simply because she was the mother of his child. With time, those feelings would deepen and evolve into love.

The possibility churned Dexter's stomach. *What if Dusty isn't ready to settle down?* Dexter couldn't remember his brother's last serious relationship. Whether Dusty was or wasn't ready to marry hardly mattered. Their father would demand Dusty live up to his responsibilities and marry the mother of his grandson—grudge or no grudge against Hank Charles.

"Figured I'd find you out here."

The words startled Dexter and he spun. "Hey, Dad," he said, surprised to see his father in the horse barn. J.W. limped forward, leaning heavily on his cane, and Dexter suspected the old rodeo injury to his leg was bothering him more than usual. "What's up?"

"Your mother tells me you've been spending a lot of time over at the Lazy S."

Dexter patted Digger's rump before leaving the stall and latching the gate. "Then I guess Mom told you I'm boarding Bud Masterson's mustang over there." He held his father's sober stare.

"Didn't we decide you had too many responsibilities with the Cottonwood horses to take on more?"

You decided. "I'm not shirking my duties around the ranch." Hell, Dusty took off to God-knows-where all the time and his parents never complained. If Dexter so much as stepped out of line once, they were all over him like buzzards on a rotting carcass.

That's because you've willingly taken on the lion's share of responsibility.

Dexter supposed he was partly to blame for his over-enthusiastic work ethic. When something needed doing, he did it—often when the chore wasn't his responsibility. Dusty once called him a control freak. Maybe his twin was right. Dexter needed to learn to delegate. The ranch hands were capable of managing the chores around the barns; they just needed the opportunity to prove themselves. "Big Ben and the others have things under control when I'm not here."

"Better use of your spare time would be practicing for the Hoedown at the end of the month." J.W. trailed Dexter through the barn, stopping when Dexter entered the storage room to check on the feed supplies.

"Little tough to practice when my partner's AWOL," Dexter said.

"Have you heard from your brother lately?"

"Nope."

"Your mother's worried about him."

Which meant his father was worried, too, although he wouldn't admit it. "I'm sure Dusty will be home soon." *Then the fireworks would go off.*

"Back to that mustang. Couldn't you have found another place to board the horse instead of the Lazy S?"

Dexter faced his father. "You've had a grudge against Hank Charles for a long time."

"We don't agree on much."

"It's more than differing philosophies. Hank insists you don't like him because he was better at rodeoing than you were in high school."

"Charles is blowing hot air."

"Is he?" Dexter paused, allowing his father a chance to admit the truth, but J.W. was a proud man and the words never came. "I saw his trophies, Dad."

J.W.'s face paled. "Is there another reason besides the mustang that you're socializing with Charles?"

"What do you mean?"

"Jesse said Josie's back in Markton with her son."

"So?"

"Your mother always believed you had a crush on that girl when Dusty dated her."

Well, heck. Apparently Dexter hadn't hidden his feelings as well as he'd believed. Why hadn't his mother ever mentioned her suspicions to him? "Josie and I are just friends." He struggled not to squirm under his father's penetrating stare.

"You sure about that?"

"There's nothing going on between us." The kiss he'd shared with Josie flashed through Dexter's mind, and heat flooded his face. He turned away before his father noticed.

"That's good. You can do better than a Charles."

Better? Wait until his father discovered his grandson was part Charles.

"Bill Chester mentioned he treated Lazy S cattle for pinkeye."

Dexter wished his father would come right out and say what was on his mind instead of blurting out single sentences. "I moved the herd closer to the house—" His father opened his mouth, but Dexter cut him off. "Seeing how Hank's still recovering from a heart attack and Josie can't handle the cattle, I thought it was the neighborly thing to do." And in case his father found fault with being neighborly, Dexter added, "I'm covering the vet bill out of my personal funds, not the ranch account."

Tense silence settled between the two men. "Is that all Charles said about me—that I never beat him at rodeo?"

"Hank hinted that there was more to the animosity between you two than a few rodeo buckles. He suggested I ask you for the details."

A mask of indifference slid over his father's face. "I don't know what he's talking about."

Figured you'd say that. There were times, like now, that Dexter believed his father kept secrets. But what secrets? Dexter had never believed the ridiculous rumors that had surfaced on and off through the years, claiming his father had had an affair early on in his marriage. J.W. was a straight arrow and a man of principle. He'd never cheat on Dexter's mother. The rumor had probably been started by a jealous person. There were plenty of people who envied the Cody wealth.

"Is there anything else you need to discuss, Dad? I'm in a rush."

"It's nine in the morning. Where are you rushing off to?"

"I'm taking Josie and her son to the rodeo in Powell."

"Thought you said you weren't involved with Hank's daughter."

"I'm not."

"Your mother and I never approved of Dusty dating her."

"I'm twenty-seven years old, Dad. You have no say in my personal relationships."

"So you are dating her," his father said.

"No, I'm not." *And yes, the kiss had been a mistake— one he wouldn't repeat.*

"Your brother came to his senses and stopped seeing that gal. You'd be wise to follow suit."

Dusty's not as perfect as you believe.

"What's going on?" Dexter's older brother Walker stepped into the barn, blocking the exit. "The ranch hands are standing outside listening in on whatever it is you two are arguing about."

"Something you need, Walker?" J.W. asked.

"I've got good news. The second well looks as if it's going to bring in the mother lode."

Walker intended to put his chemical engineering degree to work by harvesting the remaining untapped natural gas reservoirs beneath the Cottonwood Ranch and then starting the Cody Natural Gas Company. Dexter was glad his older brother had found his niche in the family business and appeared happy and content since his marriage to Paula. Time would tell if Dusty adjusted as easily as Walker had to instant fatherhood.

"That's great news." J.W.'s excitement fizzled when he switched his attention to Dexter. "Mind my words, son," he said. "She's nothing but trouble."

His father's warning about Josie rubbed Dexter raw—mostly because J.W. was right. If Dexter knew what was best for him and everyone else concerned, he'd keep his distance from Josie.

Not an easy task when the memory of her kiss set off explosions inside his head.

J.W. slapped Walker on the shoulder. "Come up to the office when you have a minute. I'd like to hear more details on the gas well." The old man shuffled from the barn, leaving the two brothers alone.

"What have you got there?" Dexter pointed to the maps in his hand.

"Something I need to show you." Walker nodded over his shoulder. "Follow me to my truck." They cut across the gravel drive.

"Where's your shadow?" Dexter asked. Even before Walker and Paula married, her two-year-old son, Clay, had developed a serious case of hero worship and had followed Walker everywhere.

"Paula drove Clay to the park in town to take his mind off his blankie."

Little Clay didn't go anywhere without his blue blankie. "What happened to his snot rag?" Dexter grinned.

"We don't know. Paula and I have looked everywhere and can't find it."

"Buy him a new one."

Walker snorted. "Wish it was that easy."

They arrived at Walker's truck and he unrolled a map and spread it across the hood.

"What am I looking at?" Dexter asked.

"A geological survey Dad had done right before he bought a huge chunk of the Lazy S Ranch back in the late eighties."

"Where'd you get this?"

"Found it hidden in the closet up at Granddad's cabin."

Dexter's business degree was of little use in attempting to decipher the symbols on the map.

"Now look at this one." Walker revealed a second map. "Notice the difference?"

"I'm no engineer. You'll have to spell it out to me."

"The second map is the same section of ranch land but shows no gas deposits. This is the survey Hank Charles commissioned."

Dexter stared at the maps, his gut churning until he felt ill. Did his father's animosity toward his neighbor run so deep that he'd use his money and power to bribe someone to alter a geological survey?

"What did Dad pay for that land?" Dexter asked.

Walker's expression sobered. "A third of what it was worth."

"No wonder Hank hates Dad." Dexter rubbed his jaw. "Remind me again why you're showing me these maps?"

"Jesse says you've been seeing a lot of Josie. Figured you might want to know what you're up against."

Just great. Everyone thought he and Josie were an item. "Josie and I are friends. There's nothing more between us." Dexter secured the maps with a rubber band. "Mind if I keep these?"

"Be my guest." Walker opened the driver's-side door and Dexter caught a flash of blue.

"Wait." Dexter felt beneath the front seat and tugged the material free. "Mystery of the missing blue blanket solved."

"Thank God." Walker gripped the security blanket as if it belonged to him. "I'd better head into town and give this to Clay." He hopped into his truck, then lowered the window. "Tell Dad I'll talk to him later about the gas wells." Walker honked and drove off.

Dexter headed for the old log-cabin-style bunkhouse, which served as the main office for ranch operations. After delivering Walker's message, he had a few questions for his father. Doris, the secretary, didn't work weekends, so Dexter walked into his father's office unannounced. J.W. looked up from the pile of papers he'd been sorting through.

"Walker found Clay's blanket and ran it into town. Said he'd catch you later to talk about the gas wells."

"That boy's too old to be dragging around a security blanket," J.W. grumbled.

"Dusty and I were five when you and Mom finally made us leave our stick horses at home when you took us on errands." Dexter sat in front of the desk.

"Maybe your mother can find your stick horse up in the attic and swap it out with the blanket next time we babysit Clay. Never too early to get my grandson interested in rodeo."

Speaking of rodeos, buckles and gas wells... "Walker found these in Grandpa's cabin." Dexter placed the maps on the desk.

J.W. glanced at the surveys. "So?"

"You said the animosity between you and Hank wasn't over rodeo." He pointed to the maps. "Is this the reason you two hate each other's guts?" *Is this the reason Josie chose not to tell Dusty about Matt or reveal Matt's birth father to her parents?*

"Are you asking me if I swindled our neighbor?"

J.W. could be a hard businessman, but as far as Dexter knew his dealings had never been unethical. "You didn't dupe Hank Charles."

"You're damned right I didn't."

"Then what happened? Why were two surveys done, and why is the one Hank commissioned missing the gas wells?"

"You'll have to ask Hank," J.W. said.

Hell. "He told me to ask you."

His father shook his head. "I don't know all the details, Dexter. Besides, what does it matter? The circumstances surrounding the sale of that land are in the past. Hank and I have both moved on. No sense digging up old bones."

Dexter suspected J.W. and Hank had not moved on and that was the reason Josie had kept Matt a secret—she feared J.W. was a threat to her and her son.

WHENEVER A NATIONAL LITTLE Britches Rodeo came to town, the event drew visitors from all over, including Canada. The Wilson County Fairgrounds were crowded with kids of all ages competing in bull riding, bareback riding, goat tying, pole bending and barrel racing. Josie's favorite nonsanctioned rodeo event was mutton bustin'.

The stands were packed with cheering spectators as little wranglers under six attempted to ride sheep. Although the kids were required to wear helmets, Josie worried her son might fall and break an arm or a leg.

Matt's pout and Dexter's I'll-keep-him-safe promise had swayed her. Now Josie sat in the bleachers and watched Dexter secure the chin strap on Matt's headgear.

"Which one's yours?" The woman seated next to Josie nodded to the throng of sheep and kids.

Josie pointed Matt out and right then Dexter glanced up and smiled.

"Wow." The woman whistled low.

"Pardon?" Josie asked.

"I can see the resemblance between father and son. *Daddy* sure is one fine-looking cowboy."

"He's my son's uncle." As soon as the words escaped her mouth Josie wanted to snatch them back.

"Well, in that case maybe I should introduce myself." The woman wiggled her bare ring finger. "I've been divorced over a year and haven't been able to land myself another husband." She smacked her chewing gum.

The woman might have been amusing if she'd been an old hag, but the platinum blonde had a Hollywood smile and a porn-star body. "He has a twin brother," Josie said. Shoot, the bimbo was more Dusty's kind of woman than Dexter's.

"You don't say…"

"Where's your son?" Josie asked.

"Daughter. She's right there."

The blond-haired child sat astride a sheep, kicking the animal with her pink cowgirl boots. Her efforts were in vain—the ewe refused to budge.

"She's awfully brave to be down there by herself," Josie said. The girl didn't look any older than Matt.

"Her daddy's with her." A long red talon pointed to a man surrounded by rodeo groupies. "You can see why we divorced." She shook her head. "Where have all the true-blue cowboys gone?"

Dexter's true-blue in every way.

Suddenly the sheep Matt sat on lurched forward and almost unseated him. Josie laughed at the shocked expression on her son's face. She hadn't seen Matt this excited since his best friend's birthday party a few months ago with the famous Clarence the Magical Clown. The mutton bustin' event was partly responsible for her son's enthusiastic mood. The other reason, she suspected, was Dexter.

Matt never stopped talking about his uncle. The other day Josie's mother had given her an odd look when Matt went on and on about how great Mr. D was.

Mr. D says one day I can ride a mustang.

Mr. D says I'm gonna grow up to be as tall as him.

Mr. D says I can be a cowboy if I want when I grow up.

Matt's nonstop *Mr. D this* and *Mr. D that* had prompted several questioning looks from her parents, which Josie had ignored.

Josie had known this day would come—when "Mom" was no longer the center of his world. She couldn't think of a better man for Matt to look up to than Dexter. In her heart she believed Dusty would eventually come around and be a part of Matt's life—then he'd have plenty of male attention.

What worried Josie was how Matt would react when they had to return to California. For a kid raised in a huge metropolis, the boy had adjusted to ranch life with ease. Matt no longer asked when his favorite shows were on TV—instead he played outside most of the day, following Dexter around the barn or watching him work with the mustang. When Dexter left, Matt would spend the rest of his time whittling with his pocketknife or practice his roping skills with her father's old rodeo rope. Bedtime was a breeze—as soon as her son's head hit the pillow, he fell asleep.

Matt had adapted to country life so thoroughly and in such a short time that Josie questioned whether she knew what was best for her son. She'd convinced herself that California was a great place to raise a child. In truth, her own selfish wants and desires kept them in Santa Monica. She loved the sunshine. The ocean. The crowds and the festivals. Loved the variety of restaurants and ethnic foods. But Matt loved Wyoming and deserved to be near family.

Did she dare consider returning to Markton? She'd have no trouble working remotely for corporations and lawyers who needed documentation of depositions and other business meetings and events. Once the Codys and her parents learned Dusty was Matt's father would her and Matt's presence create even more tension between the families or allow them to mend their differences and put the past to rest? Her father's weak heart didn't need any more stress.

"Mom, look at me!" Matt's shout ended Josie's fretting.

She waved and blew him a kiss. Dexter patted the sheep's rump and the animal jumped forward, then turned sideways quickly and Matt tumbled to the ground. Dexter grabbed Matt by the seat of his jeans and swung him through the air and onto the back of another sheep. The animal trotted off and Dexter held on to Matt's belt loop as he jogged alongside. Josie wished she'd thought to bring a camera today.

A few minutes later a loud buzzer sounded, signaling a rest period for the livestock. The kids removed their helmets and exited the pen. Josie turned to say goodbye to the woman next to her, but the beauty queen had disappeared.

"Did you see, Mom? Did you see? I rode a sheep," Matt said, when Josie met up with them.

"You were terrific, honey." She hugged her son, but he squirmed loose after a few seconds. "Mr. D says I can play the fishing game next."

Mr. D. Soon Matt would call Dexter "Uncle Dex." "Okay, then." She ruffled her son's hair. "Off to the fishing pond." They moseyed along the fairgrounds, Matt a few steps ahead. Dexter quieter than usual. "Is something wrong?" she asked.

"No. Why?" His terse response convinced her there was more going on in his mind than showing her and Matt a good time.

"You've barely looked me in the eye all morning," she said. Did he regret their kiss? Was that why he'd brought Ricky with him all week when he'd shown up at the Lazy S to do chores and work with the mustang— because he didn't want to be alone with her?

"Your dad showed me his rodeo trophies the other day."

Dexter sure had become best buddies with her father.

"Seems your dad beat the pants off mine in rodeo competitions during high school." Dexter grinned.

"Dad's a fighter. My grandfather took off when Dad was a little kid and my grandmother had barely kept a roof over my father's head. Dad had to scratch out a place for himself in life. It's tough to beat sheer determination."

Josie had a hunch their fathers' fierce rivalry wasn't the reason Dexter refused to make eye contact. "What else did my father say about J.W.?"

Dexter's blue eyes turned cloudy. With worry? "Do you think there's another reason why—aside from rodeo—our fathers don't get along?"

Oh, boy. Had Dexter discovered J.W. had swindled her father out of valuable land? A lot of years had passed, and she wondered if both men hadn't twisted the facts in their minds. Not wanting to dig up the past when they were having an enjoyable afternoon, she said, "Let's not discuss our fathers—they're both frustrating men."

They reached the line for the fishing game. "Can I watch up there?" Matt pointed to the counter where carnival workers attached magnets to the kids' fishing lines.

"Sure, but stand where I can see you," Josie said.

They moved forward in the line and Josie's boot heel came down on a rock. Her ankle twisted and she teetered. Dexter steadied her with a hand on her arm. "Thanks." Their gazes clung and her breathing grew labored. Right then she decided he hadn't regretted their kiss—not when his eyes threatened to devour her in broad daylight.

He released his grip on her arm and cleared his throat. "Have you decided when you're returning to California?"

"Dad sees the doctor next week. If he gets the all-clear sign, I'll take off at the end of the month." *Unless you give me a reason to stay.* "Have you heard from Dusty?"

The muscle along Dexter's jaw bunched. "No."

"Don't worry, Dex. Your brother'll figure things out." If Dusty didn't come home soon, then Josie would speak to the Codys herself about Matt.

A few minutes later they reached the front of the line, and she stepped aside to watch Dexter and Matt strategize how to catch one of the bigger prizes in the pond. Matt said something that made Dexter laugh, and Josie was seduced by the cowboy all over again. As far as she was concerned, the day couldn't go by fast enough. She wanted to return to the Lazy S where she hoped to coax another kiss from Dexter.

"I'M GONNA SHOW GRANDMA and Grandpa my new rope," Matt said when Dexter parked in the Lazy S ranch yard. "Thanks, Mr. D." Matt leaned over the front seat and squeezed Dexter's neck.

"Sure thing, buddy. Glad you had a good time."

"Tell Grandma I'll be right in." Once Matt shut the truck door, Josie asked, "Are you staying to check on Zeus?"

"I'd planned to. Why?"

"Nothing." She smiled.

They got out of the truck, and Josie followed Dexter to the round pen. "I'll get his food." She retreated inside the barn where Dexter had left grain for the horse. While she filled the feed bins and added fresh water to the trough, Dexter entered the corral.

He spoke in low tones and the horse's ears perked. Then she watched in amazement as the mustang moved forward and nudged Dexter's shoulder with his nose. Dexter reached into his pocket for a sugar cube. The stallion ate the treat and trotted off.

"When do you think you'll be able to ride him?" she asked.

"I'll bring a saddle over on Monday and see how he reacts." Dexter latched the gate behind him.

Josie didn't want him to leave. "Come into the barn. I have something for you." She entered first, then retreated into the shadows and waited.

"What is it?" Dexter stepped through the doors.

"This." Josie slid her hand around his neck, stood on tiptoes and pressed her mouth to Dexter's.

Taken by surprise, he froze. Josie slipped her tongue into his mouth, then took him on a wet, exhilarating ride. When she ended the kiss, they were both panting.

"Where in the world did you learn to kiss like that?" he asked, eyes warm with passion. "Never mind, I don't want to know."

Lips tingling, Josie inched closer. A kiss wasn't enough anymore—she wanted to make love with Dexter.

"Josie, we need to talk." He backed up a step.

The barn was no place to make love. What if her father or Matt had walked in on them? Good grief—all her common sense disappeared around Dexter.

"Thanks for making this day special for Matt and me." Rising on tiptoe, she kissed his cheek, then left him alone in the barn. She had some serious thinking to do about her and Matt's future.

Chapter Nine

Dexter's kiss lingered on her mind when Josie entered the house. As soon as she closed the door she hurried to the front window and watched his truck drive away.

"The last time you had that dreamy look on your face Dusty had just asked you out on a date."

"Hi, Mom." Not in the mood to discuss her and Dexter's relationship, Josie said, "I'd better get Matt ready for bed."

"Your father's got him in the tub. Come into the kitchen and keep me company while I wash the supper dishes." Her mother walked off before Josie had a chance to protest.

Might as well get this over with. Once in the kitchen she went straight to the refrigerator. "Iced tea?"

"Sure. I'll have a glass." Pots and pans clanged. Cupboards opened and closed.

Josie poured two glasses of tea, then sat at the table. "Matt had a great time today."

"I know." Her mother glanced over her shoulder. "He wouldn't stop talking about Mr. D."

Nothing new there.

"Only this time," her mother continued, her voice dropping a decibel, "he said he wished Mr. D was his dad."

Oh, dear. She'd known Matt was becoming attached to Dexter but hadn't realized he'd viewed his uncle as a potential father. If only her son realized how close he'd come to choosing his real father. "Did Dad flip his lid?"

Her mother rolled her eyes. "In all the years he's been your father have you ever seen him *flip* his *lid?*"

"No." Mostly her father resorted to giving the offender the silent treatment. She squirmed under her mother's pointed stare. "What?"

"You're an adult and it's none of my business who you become involved with—" her mother held up her hand when Josie attempted to speak "—but your first responsibility is to your son."

"I know that." Hadn't she raised Matt by herself the past four…almost five years?

"You have to protect him from getting his feelings hurt."

"No one's going to hurt him, Mom."

"How do you suppose he'll feel when you pack your bags and return to California?"

Josie had asked herself that question a million times over since arriving in Wyoming.

"Not until your father and I visited you in L.A. after you'd enrolled in college out there did we realize how much you'd changed. You were happier in California than you'd ever been in Markton. How will you adjust to small-town life again if—"

"You're jumping to conclusions. No one said anything about me and Matt moving back here."

"Dexter sure isn't going to relocate to the West Coast."

Were her feelings for Dexter that obvious? Josie stood. "This is none of your business, Mom."

"You've already had your heart broken by one Cody."

That was just it—Dusty hadn't broken her heart. But Dexter—this Cody cowboy was another story. He had the potential to wreak havoc on her heart. Yet the threat of a broken heart didn't deter her from wanting to make love to Dexter. "Don't worry. I'm a big girl."

"Even big girls make mistakes, honey."

With her mother's words ringing in her ears, Josie left the room in search of a distraction. She didn't want to weigh the pros and cons of becoming romantically involved with a Cody—mostly because there were too many cons. What she really yearned to do was lose herself in Dexter and not worry about what tomorrow might bring.

AH, HELL.

Dexter pulled on Digger's reins and the horse slowed to a halt. "Ricky, you've gotta turn the steer to the left sooner," he called across the practice ring.

"Shoot, boss, I'm no header." Ricky swung his mount around and followed Dexter back to the starting boxes.

The Missoula Hoedown was Saturday. Dexter wanted to make sure Digger wasn't favoring his front leg anymore, so he'd coerced Ricky into playing Dusty's role in team roping. Digger's leg was the least of Dexter's

problems. He had five days to prepare for the rodeo—
not an easy task when half the roping team remained
missing.

Last night he'd phoned Dusty, and as was the norm,
his brother's voice mailbox was full. Timing was everything in team roping. If Dexter and Dusty didn't perfect
their moves, both as a team and with their respective
horses, they could kiss their chances of winning the
event goodbye. Losing was out of the question. Josie
planned to attend the hoedown with Matt and he wanted
to impress them with a win.

Earlier that morning he'd dropped by the Lazy S to
work with Zeus and discovered Josie waiting by the
corral with a hot thermos of coffee. For a few minutes they'd stood side by side sharing the coffee while
they watched the stallion eat his oats. Sexual tension
had sizzled between them, but he'd kept a respectable
distance from her, avoiding any accidental brushes or
smoldering looks.

When the temptation to touch her had become too
much, Dexter had retreated inside the pen and spent
the next two hours attempting to saddle Zeus. By the
end of the training session, the stallion had only tol-
erated a saddle blanket over his back. When Dexter
had departed, he'd issued Josie an invitation to drop
by the Cottonwood Ranch later in the day for a tour of
the horse barns. He glanced at his watch. The afternoon was slipping away, and Josie had yet to make an
appearance.

Maybe she'd changed her mind because she hadn't
wanted to chance running into his parents. He shouldn't
have invited her in the first place, but Josie was wearing
down his defenses one smile at a time. After another

practice run with Ricky, he'd phone Josie and inform her that his folks had flown to Harrison, Idaho, to view a stallion at the famous Black Rock Ranch. He'd rather be with Josie on his home turf. Nothing could happen between them with a ranch full of cowboys wandering around.

"You two want another steer loaded in the chute?" Slim's question grabbed Dexter's attention.

He nodded to the ranch hand. "One more time, Ricky."

"Whatever you say, boss."

Dexter and Ricky entered their respective boxes on either side of the chute. Slim attached a breakaway barrier to the steer and stretched it across the open end of the header's box where Ricky sat astride his horse, Maverick.

"Ready?" Dexter asked.

"Don't have much choice, do—" The rest of the cowboy's words were cut short when the steer broke free and crossed the score line, which released the barrier. Maverick shot out of the chute, almost unseating Ricky. Digger responded to Maverick's move and trailed slightly behind. From there everything slid downhill.

Ricky threw his rope and missed the steer's head. Maverick chased the steer and Digger, confused, slammed on the brakes, sending Dexter flying over his head into the dirt.

"Sorry 'bout that, boss," Ricky said.

Feminine laughter met Dexter's ears as he crawled to his feet. Josie stood outside the corral, one boot propped on the bottom rung. "Better luck next time, cowboy."

"Who's that?" Ricky whistled between his teeth.

"Josie Charles. Instead of gawking at her, you should thank her."

"For what?"

"For showing up when she did or else I'd have beaten the crap out of you."

"In that case, ma'am, thank you." Ricky tipped his hat.

"My pleasure." Josie's pretty brown eyes sparkled.

She'd done something different to her hair since Dexter had seen her earlier in morning. The bright sun intensified the red highlights and he clenched his gloved hand into a fist to keep from tugging on the curls that fell to her shoulders.

"Wasn't sure you'd show up." He kept his voice low in deference to Slim's and Ricky's big ears.

"I waited for Matt to go down for a nap."

Her smile jolted him. How easy it would be to lose himself in Josie and forget about the consequences.

"We finished, boss?" Slim asked.

His attention fixated on Josie's mouth, Dexter said, "Yeah. We're taking a break."

"Figured." Slim roped the steer and led the animal into a holding pen with other livestock used for training the cow horses.

Dexter grabbed Digger's reins and clicked his tongue. The horse followed him out of the corral. "Let me ask one of the hands to put Digger up, then I'll show you the infamous Mr. Lucky Son."

After a short walk to the barn, Dexter handed Digger's reins to Paco, who nodded politely to Josie before leading the horse to a stall. Halfway to the stallion barn, Dexter's sister, Elly, interrupted. "Dex, wait up!"

Elly trotted along the paved driveway, her blond ponytail swishing across her back. "Josie?" she said when she drew close. "Josie Charles, is that you?"

"In the flesh. Hi, Ellen."

Elly's gaze bounced between Josie and Dexter. "How's your dad feeling?"

"He's much better, thanks."

"I haven't seen you since you graduated from high school."

"I live in Santa Monica now."

"Really? Would you be willing to do an interview for my blog?"

"Whoa, Elly, you're doing it again." His sister had a habit of ambushing ranch visitors and badgering them for interviews.

"What kind of blog?" Josie asked.

"Cottonwood Chronicles. I write about ranch life. I have a large following, and I know my readers would love to hear more about California."

Josie chuckled. "My life isn't as glamorous as the movies."

"I'm sure that's not true."

Dexter crossed his arms over his chest and swallowed his irritation. Might as well give in to Elly now, or she'd buzz around them like a pesky horsefly until she obtained the information she wanted.

"Well, the Santa Monica Pier is fun and I love living near the ocean," Josie said.

"Have you been to a gallery called the Fig?"

"Once."

Elly elbowed Dexter in the gut. "Bergamot Station has the single greatest concentration of art galleries in Santa Monica."

So?

"I wish I could get my ranch photographs into one of those galleries. Or have my own booth during the film festival in November."

While Josie and his sister chatted, Dexter's thoughts drifted along a serious path. He stared northeast toward Carter Mountain and higher to the summit where the Shoshone National Forest began. He loved the wild beauty of the mountains. But how would they stand up against constant sunshine, sandy beaches and ocean waves? There were no *piers* with carnival rides out here—only rodeos. As for retail shopping…the mall in Cody couldn't compare to the upscale stores in Josie's neck of the woods.

A pit formed in his stomach. Santa Monica was a world away from Markton, Wyoming. Josie had left Markton because she'd wanted change—a different lifestyle. There was nothing in Markton to keep her here—except Dusty.

And me. Dexter's feelings for Josie were a tangled mess. He didn't know which was worse—the idea of Josie returning to California or staying in Markton and making a life with Dusty.

"Here's my card." Elly dug out a business card from her pocket and handed it to Josie. "E-mail me when you get back to Santa Monica and I'll send you a list of questions I use for interviews. It'll be fun."

"My mother mentioned seeing your prints at the Tangled Antlers Gallery."

"Photographs from my Cottonwood Collection."

"Mom was very impressed."

Elly snapped her fingers. "You should tag along with me and Janie Hansen—you remember Mark Hansen's sister?—on our next girls' day out. We're making plans to fly to Sheridan to a new day spa that's gotten rave reviews. Maybe you can join us."

"Elly…" Dexter scowled.

"Sorry." His sister smiled sheepishly. "I tend to hijack conversations." She motioned to the barn. "Is Dex taking you to see Mr. Lucky Son?"

"Yes," Dexter answered for Josie. "Now bug off."

"I used to get into trouble for tagging along after my brothers." Elly winked at Josie. "Remember the time I found you and Mary Francis kissing behind the bleachers during the football game?"

"Mary Francis?" Josie's mouth dropped open. "Didn't her mother send her to a private girls' school out East after her sophomore year?"

"They were afraid Dex would steal her virginity." Elly snickered.

"Oh, for God's sake." Dexter shook his head. "It was one kiss."

"Dusty never said a word about you dating Mary Francis," Josie said.

"Dusty didn't know." Elly pointed her finger at Dexter. "He bullied me into keeping his secret."

"I *paid* you to keep your mouth shut." Dexter had given his sister a dollar a day to forget what she saw. Obviously he'd wasted his money.

Right then a horn honked, drawing the group's attention. "Oh, look, it's Nicki Sable."

"What's she doing here?" Dexter asked.

Ignoring him, Elly spoke to Josie. "Nicki's the girl Jesse took to the senior prom." Elly waved a hand in the air at the pretty, blond-haired, green-eyed woman who stepped from the truck. "Anyway, she and Jesse are still good friends." Elly pointed to the stock trailer hitched to the back of the pickup. "Jesse said Nicki might be bringing over a bull from her father's herd for him to practice on today if she got out of work early."

"Tell Big Ben to put the bull in a pen by himself," Dexter told his sister.

Elly's cell phone rang and she glanced at the number. "It's Stella calling from the gallery. Maybe I sold a photograph." She answered the phone and walked off to greet Nicki.

"Sorry about that," he said. "Elly's a pest." Hoping to avoid another interruption, Dexter grabbed Josie's hand and walked at a fast clip toward the stallion barn.

"I like your sister. She's spunky."

"Yeah, she's spunky, all right." Dexter held open a door at the back of the barn and motioned for Josie to precede him into the building.

"Dusty used to complain about you."

"Me?" Dexter stopped outside his mother's office.

"He said you were nosy."

Dexter snorted and Josie giggled. "Is it true that after Dusty came home from one of our dates you would ask him what base he got to with me?"

Okay, so he had been nosy. He'd had a crush on Josie and imagining his brother kissing her, touching her in places Dexter wanted to touch her had darn near killed him.

"I don't know what Dusty told you," Josie said. "But I held out a long time before I had sex with him. I probably wouldn't have slept with him at all if I didn't fear he'd dump me for a girl who would."

Yeah, that sounded like something his brother would do, but in his brother's defense, there were plenty of girls back then willing to put out for Dusty.

"And there was another reason I slept with your brother."

Dexter didn't care to talk about his twin, but Josie appeared determined to rehash the past. "And what was that?"

"I worried that if I broke up with Dusty, you and I would no longer be friends." She clasped his hand. "I didn't want to lose your friendship, Dex."

Guilt flooded him. Josie had lost his friendship not because of anything she'd done but because Dexter hadn't been able to handle his jealousy. Had he even crossed Josie's mind the night she'd slept with Dusty and conceived Matt? He doubted it.

"C'mon. I'll show you where Mom keeps her stallions." To his knowledge Josie had never been inside any of the Cottonwood barns. Because their parents had disapproved of Dusty dating her, his brother had rarely brought Josie to the ranch.

"Wow." Josie's eyes widened. "The stalls are huge."

Each stallion had a sixteen-by-twenty custom stall.

Josie wandered closer and read the information sheet that hung on the outside of one solid oak door. Right then Black Duce Two kicked the side of the stall and Josie squawked.

"Careful. Black Duce has a temper." Dexter led Josie along the row of stalls and stopped at the end. "This is Mr. Lucky Sun." The horse ignored their presence, his head stuck out the open window on the other side of the stall.

"He's gorgeous." The horse sported a dark brown coat with a white blaze down his face.

"In here," Dexter said, "is our state-of-the-art reproduction facility." He and Josie entered a large sterile laboratory. "Mom's staff identifies embryos and prepares them for transfer and does semen evaluations and processing for cooled transport or freezing."

"This is really high-tech." Josie ran a finger across the edge of the stainless-steel table with several microscope stations.

"And this is the semen collection room." Dexter opened another door and Josie moved past him, the scent of her shampoo trailing behind her. The sweet fragrance made Dexter wish they were anywhere but here.

He opened another door. "This is our surgical suite used for embryo transfers, insemination and standing reproductive surgeries."

"How much of your day do you spend in here?" she asked.

"None. I don't have anything to do with Mom's breeding program." They retraced their steps through the lab. "I'll show you where I spend most of my time." They left the stallion barn and cut across the drive, past the round pens and the remote-controlled roping chutes. When they entered the barn they ran into Slim.

The ranch hand tipped his hat. "Ma'am."

"I'm giving Josie a tour of the barn." Ignoring Slim's quizzical expression, Dexter placed his fingers against the small of her back and escorted her down the center aisle. "This barn is home to the working horses, the yearlings and our family's and ranch hands' personal mounts." When Josie stared quizzically at the empty stalls, Dexter said, "Most of the horses are out in the pastures or being worked with by the hands.

"Feed storage room is at the front of the barn." Dexter motioned behind them. "This is the tack room." He opened the door and Josie poked her head inside.

"What's in there?" She pointed to the closed door across from the tack room.

"The playroom."

"Let me see." Josie opened the door and gasped. "A mechanical bull?"

Dexter closed the door behind them. "When Jesse turned ten, he told our parents he wanted to be the best bull rider in the world. Our father went out that day and purchased a mechanical bull. That one broke years ago. This is the fourth one we've had at the ranch."

Josie stepped over the mats to get a closer look at the machine. "Can I try?" Her flirty smile had trouble written all over it.

Why not? "Hop on." He walked over to the control unit mounted on the wall and flipped the switch to the lowest setting. The machine jerked, then began a subtle twisting motion while raising and lowering in the air.

Grinning, Dexter said, "Lift your right arm above your head." He immediately regretted his words. When Josie raised her arm the action pulled her Western blouse tight across her breasts, showing off their size and shape.

"I think I'm ready for more," she said.

You're not the only one. Unable to tear his attention from her swaying body, Dexter flipped the switch to the next level and the bull rocked at a steeper angle.

"Ooh… This is fun."

His mouth turned to cotton as he watched her body twist and stretch. Like an erotic dancer, her breasts thrust out, then in, teasing and taunting him. The bull dipped forward sharply and Josie's fanny lifted in the air. Arousal swift and sharp swept through Dexter, carrying his imagination along for the ride. An image of him and Josie sitting astride the rocking bull sans clothing flashed before his eyes and he groaned.

Watching no longer satisfied Dexter. He flipped the switch back to level one and slid behind Josie on the bull, his thighs bracketing her hips. The next time the bull dipped, her breath hitched—the quietest of gasps— when his arousal pressed hard against her fanny. He caressed her flat tummy, then trailed his fingers up her side and along the arm she held in the air.

"Mmm…" Josie leaned back, her head resting on his shoulder. He nuzzled her neck, inhaling her perfume, the tempting scent of her skin. "You're making me crazy, Dex."

"Then we're even, because you're driving me insane." She turned her head and he captured her lips. Never before had he been this attuned to a woman. Her heat and softness sucked him under like quicksand and with each rocking motion of the bull Dexter flirted with the point of no return.

He nibbled her earlobe. "Want me to stop?"

Josie sighed, the whisper of air rising from the depths of her soul. *Stop?* "Never."

Chapter Ten

You're playing with fire, man.

One more touch, then Dexter would stop.

The rocking motion of the mechanical bull forced his body against Josie's in places he'd only dreamed of touching these past few weeks. He freed the buttons on her blouse and stroked warm, quivering flesh. Closing his eyes, he let his senses consume him. How many nights had he lain awake in bed, his mind racing with fantasies of making love to this woman? Those dreams hadn't come close to the reality of here and now.

This is wrong. Stop.

"I'm hot." Josie's breath caressed his neck and a groan of pleasure exploded from Dexter's gut. Her touch was torture. Teasing…taunting…begging him to cross the line with her.

Feeling torn inside, Dexter's brain chastised him for touching Josie this way, but his heart insisted here and now—this moment—was all they'd ever have.

You know there can never be anything more between you.

Ignoring the voice in his head, Dexter stroked Josie's bare midriff…toyed with the strap of her pink bra… cupped her breasts. He nuzzled her neck, inhaling the erotic scent of her skin. She arched her back, pressing his hands tighter to her breasts. Deep in his heart he believed his feelings for Josie were good, right and permissible.

Josie was *the one*.

The one for Dusty—not you.

Bitter jealousy stirred Dexter as he kissed a path down the back of Josie's neck. He'd stood on the sidelines in high school while his twin had taken what Dexter had wanted for himself—Josie. That he had to step aside a second time was killing him.

Her hands moved restlessly over his thighs and all thoughts of right or wrong vanished. When the bull dipped forward, her nails bit into his leg muscle to keep her balance. "More, Dex."

"Anything you want, babe." Hands and fingers teased. Zippers, buttons and snaps came undone. Then Josie faced him, straddling his thighs. He kissed her, wanting…no, *needing* to show her that he was more involved with her than just physically. He stared into her brown eyes, bright with desire—and saw Dusty's face.

A cold knot formed in Dexter's chest. Josie, Dusty and Matt had a chance to be a real family—what right did Dexter have to take that from them? What would his father say about Dexter's actions today? More important—how could Dexter face Dusty with a clean conscience after making love with Josie?

Dexter had to put a stop to his insane obsession with Josie. Dusty was family—more than family, he was Dexter's twin. Dexter wasn't willing to destroy his relationship with Dusty or his family because he couldn't control his impulses around Josie.

With a strength he hadn't known he possessed, Dexter dived off the bull and landed on the mats. Sucking in deep breaths, he stared at the wood rafters crisscrossing the ceiling. He'd barely gotten himself under control before Josie launched herself on top of him.

"I want you, Dex." She nuzzled his chin.

Josie's declaration cut him off at the knees, and with concentrated effort he tucked her beneath him and stretched her arms above her head, locking her wrists within his grasp—afraid if he released her he'd cave and give her what she wanted—what both of them wanted. "We can't do this."

"If you're worried about protection—"

"No, it's not that."

Undeterred, Josie wiggled loose and coaxed Dexter onto his back, then straddled his waist. The torment in his blue eyes stole her breath. She brushed a strand of sweaty hair off his forehead. "I know you're attracted to me. I know you want me. So what's wrong?" When he refused to speak, she threatened, "I'll kiss you, if you don't fess up."

Instead of words he chose action—moving her off him. He rose from the mats and retreated to the opposite side of the room, leaving the still-gyrating bull between them. His anguished expression tore at her heart. "I thought you wanted this?" Her words sounded cold and stilted in the muggy room.

Chest heaving, Dexter dropped his gaze to the ground, unwilling to reveal the demons that tormented him. Feeling vulnerable and foolish, Josie buttoned her blouse and straightened her clothing.

"I do want you, Josie." Dexter's guttural confession reached deep inside her and tugged.

"I don't understand."

"Just let it be."

"Don't I get a say in our relationship?" she asked.

"We don't have a relationship."

What? Dexter might as well have slapped her, his words stung so deeply. "You're telling me that our quiet talks in the morning when you train the mustang, our outings with Matt…the fishing…the fair, our kisses… all meant nothing to you?" His silence fed Josie's ire. "If we don't have a relationship, then why are you spending so much time with me and Matt?"

"Someone has to look after you until Dusty returns."

Hurt, she lashed out. "Do you always kiss and grope your charges?" *Blast it!* Dexter made her mad enough to spit.

He flipped the switch on the wall and the bucking machine's motor groaned to a halt. Even in her anger, Josie's attraction to Dexter reared its ugly head. His shirttail stuck out of his jeans and his belt buckle hung askew—the cowboy looked sexy as all get-out and the last thing she wanted to do was leave the room without finishing what they'd started.

"I accept full blame for letting things get out of hand between us," Dexter said.

"Don't talk like that. I'm a grown woman. If I want to make love to a man, I can. I for darn sure don't need anyone making excuses for me."

The muscle along Dexter's jaw bunched, spurring Josie across the room. "Don't," she said, straightening his belt buckle.

"Don't what?"

She softened her tone of voice. "Don't overanalyze what just happened. Let it be." *Because I'm crazy for you. And I want to see where whatever is happening between us leads.*

The sound of footsteps reached their ears.

"We'd better leave before someone notices how long we've been in here," he said.

A shiver of unease rippled through her body, and she couldn't shake the feeling that once they left their secret hideaway, nothing would ever be the same.

"Hang on a sec." He undid the top buttons of her blouse, his knuckles brushing against her breasts. Her pulse raced. A change of heart? Then he dashed her hopes. "Your buttons are crooked."

"Oh." Her pounding heart slowed to a dull thump.

Dexter opened the door and ushered her out. She came face-to-face with Slim. The ranch hand tipped his hat.

"I was showing Josie the mechanical bull," Dexter mumbled.

"Wondered what was making all that ruckus in there."

Face flaming, Josie pretended interest in a horse named Candy Cane while Dexter and Slim exchanged a few words.

"Is Ricky working with the yearlings?" Dexter's deep voice held a note of warning. If Slim was smart, he wouldn't utter a word about the *noises* he'd overheard.

"Yup. He's out there now," Slim said.

"I'm heading over to the Lazy S to check on the mustang."

Josie released a deep breath, relieved that Dexter wasn't running from her. On the heels of relief came apprehension—did he want to be with her because he felt obligated to? Or because he wanted to?

"Josie?"

She whirled. "What?"

"Ready?" Dexter's empty-eyed stare glanced off her face.

Josie nodded. Side by side they strolled through the barn. The backs of their hands accidentally brushed and she curled her pinkie finger around his. Hope blossomed in her chest when he squeezed back. *Everything's going to be okay.*

"I've been looking all over for you, Dex."

Dexter skidded to a halt. A cold band of pressure cinched his chest, leaving him speechless.

Dusty had returned.

Afraid to look at Josie for fear his brother would guess what they'd been doing only moments ago in the barn, Dexter released Josie's finger and asked, "When did you get back?"

"Just now." Dusty glanced between Josie and Dexter. "Josie."

"Hello, Dusty."

Frowning, Dusty asked, "Where's Mom and Dad?"

"They hopped a flight to Idaho a few hours ago." Dexter shifted his stance, adding another foot of space between him and Josie.

"What are you doing here?" Dusty directed the question to Josie. "Matt's not with you, is he?"

"He's not here," Dexter answered. "I offered to give Josie a tour of the ranch."

"You sure that's all you were up to?" Dusty nodded to Josie.

Panic gnawed a hole in Dexter's bravado while guilt slammed into him from all sides. He struggled to make eye contact with his brother. Had Dusty guessed that Dexter had almost made love to Josie? Even if Dusty suspected the two had gotten out of line, Dexter refused to allow his brother to badger Josie. "What are you insinuating?"

"I'm asking if you invited Josie here to spill the beans to Mom and Dad about Matt."

Relieved Dusty hadn't suspected foul play between him and Josie, Dexter muttered, "That's low, Dusty. We stood by our promise even though you took your sweet ol' time coming home."

"Sorry." Dusty whipped off his hat and spun it on the tip of his middle finger. He opened his mouth, then snapped it closed.

"Spit it out, Dusty," Dexter said. The sooner this confrontation ended, the safer for all parties involved.

"Okay. Look. I've given this a lot of thought."

"Given what thought?" Josie asked.

"I think the best thing to do in our situation is to get married."

Married? Blindsided, Dexter stopped breathing. *You believed all along that marriage was the best solution for all parties involved.* True, but deep down Dexter had held out hope that his brother would tuck tail and run from doing the right thing.

Dusty paced—five steps forward, then five steps back—gravel dust billowing around his boot heels. "I'm ready to be a father to Matt."

Dexter felt like bellowing.

"I never doubted that you'd want to be Matt's father," Josie said. "But marriage is a little extreme."

Josie's eyes burned a hole into the side of Dexter's head—might as well have been a bullet, her stare was so painful. His brother's honest-to-God sincere expression stopped Dexter from coming to Josie's defense. *Shit.* For the first time in his life Dusty wanted to put others before himself.

Just like old times...his brother got the girl. *Again.*

Everything inside Dexter wanted to be Matt's father and Josie's husband. But Dexter couldn't live with himself if he stood in Dusty's way. He'd expect the same loyalty from Dusty if their positions were reversed. There was only one thing left to do. Dexter had to forget his feelings for Josie and his dreams for a future with her.

"If we don't marry, people will talk," Dusty said.

"You Codys have been the subject of gossip all your lives." Josie propped her hands on her hips and glared. "Since when have people's comments ever bothered you?"

"This doesn't just affect me. It affects my whole family." Dusty smacked Dexter's arm. "Right?"

"Right." The word sounded strangled to Dexter's ears.

"And I'm saying who cares what others say or think about Dusty being Matt's father," Josie said.

She stared expectantly at Dexter, and it killed him that he couldn't...no, *wouldn't* come to her defense. "Dusty's right. The gossip might hurt Matt."

"See, Josie. Dexter thinks it's a good idea, too." Dusty set his hat on his head. "When you and Matt move back to Markton, tongues are gonna wag."

"Hold up. I haven't agreed to move anywhere," Josie said.

Dusty frowned. "If we marry, then you'll have to live here."

"No." She stamped her boot.

"No, what?" Dusty asked.

"No, I won't marry you. No, I won't leave California and move here."

"At least say you'll consider my proposal."

"All right." Josie straightened her shoulders. "I'll consider your proposal."

What the hell had happened to "No, I won't marry you"? Dexter glanced at Josie and the stark pain in her eyes cut him like a knife.

"Fair enough," Dusty said. "I'd like to tell my folks about Matt when they return from Idaho later tonight."

"Tomorrow." Spinning on her boot heels Josie stomped to her truck. Apparently, she'd had enough of the Cody brothers.

"I'll call you later!" Dusty yelled.

With a wave of her hand Josie acknowledged that she'd heard Dusty.

A sick feeling attacked Dexter's gut. He'd told himself over and over these past weeks to keep his distance from Josie, but all he'd gotten for his efforts was an ulcer. He knew there could never be anything between them, yet he'd dreamed they'd had a future. He'd allowed himself to care. To risk his heart again. Damn it, he'd gone and done the unthinkable—he'd fallen in love with Josie.

Never mind that Josie belonged with Dusty.

Never mind that Dexter was racked with so much guilt he could barely look his brother in the eye.

Never mind that he'd put his wants and desires before what was best for his own flesh and blood.

Dexter had to end this foolish fantasy he'd built up in his head. Dusty was his brother. His twin. His best friend. No matter how he yearned to be with Josie he didn't dare let her come between him and his twin.

"Dex, what's wrong?" Dusty asked.

"Nothing." *Everything.* Dexter stomped off, before he said or did something he'd surely regret.

"NICE WHEELS," JOSIE SAID when she hopped into the front seat of Dusty's white Ford F-350. The inside was spotless and still had that new-car smell.

"Sit."

"I am," Josie said.

"Sorry, not you." Dusty reached over the backseat and opened the window in the middle of the rear windshield. "Sit, Track."

Josie noted the Border collie obeyed. Dusty had another think coming if he believed she'd obey and marry him.

Dusty shifted into Reverse. "Ready?"

Was anyone ever ready to face a firing squad? "I guess."

Dusty had offered to pick her up this morning so they could discuss their game plan for revealing that Matt was a Cody.

Game plan. Good grief. Did men always equate difficult situations to sports?

As they drove away Josie's eyes shifted to the barn. Dexter was in the corral with Zeus, attempting to put a saddle on him. When he'd arrived earlier in the morning he hadn't bothered to stop at the house and apologize for being a big chicken and not telling his brother that he had feelings for her.

Yesterday when Dexter hadn't objected to Dusty's marriage proposal, her heart had splintered into a million pieces. The encounter brought back painful memories of high school when Dexter had turned his back on her.

"About you and Matt moving to Markton…" Dusty said, snagging her attention.

If Dexter had proposed to her, she'd have relocated to Wyoming in a heartbeat. "You're asking me to give up my job, leave the only home Matt has ever known, his friends, his school—"

"We're all making sacrifices, Josie."

Ouch. Evidently Dusty's sacrifice was settling for *her.*

He selected a music CD from the holder attached to the passenger-seat visor. Dierks Bentley sang "What Was I Thinkin'" and Josie wondered the exact same thing when she'd agreed to consider Dusty's marriage proposal.

"Have you given more thought to—"

"C'mon, Dusty. You can't be serious. We don't love each other."

He shrugged. "We had fun together in California."

Fun was one thing. *Forever* would be a life sentence to a man like Dusty. Besides, being with Dexter these past few weeks only reaffirmed how wrong she and Dusty were for each other. Granted, lots of couples entered into marriage as friends and with time developed a lasting affection for each other. But Josie refused to settle for less than a fairy-tale ending.

Dusty's intentions might be honorable, but they'd end up divorcing inside of a year. One day Dusty would settle down with the right woman—but now wasn't the time and she wasn't that woman. In truth, she liked Dusty just the way he was—a cowboy Casanova. She didn't care to change him. And why should he change for her when she didn't love him and never would? No matter which angle she viewed the situation from, she and Dusty *together* was wrong. Plain wrong.

"You didn't tell your parents anything, did you?" he asked.

"Nope." Josie had ignored the concerned look her mother and father had exchanged over the breakfast table when she'd announced that Dusty was taking her for a drive this morning. She'd sat in the rocker on the front porch and had waited for Dusty—her eyes following Dexter's every move. She'd wanted him to give her a sign that he was aware she and Dusty were about to drop a bomb on the Cody family. *Nothing*. He hadn't even glanced in her direction.

"Nervous?" Dusty white-knuckled the steering wheel—obviously he was strung tighter than barbed wire.

"Not really." Josie spoke the truth. Late last night she'd arrived at the realization that no matter what happened today, one fact would remain constant—she'd always be Matt's mother. Sharing her son with the Cody clan and Dusty wouldn't change that. Her worry that

J.W. would take Matt away from her had been based on an unfounded fear, and she was ashamed she'd kept Matt from his family for so long.

"Josie?"

"Yeah?"

Several seconds ticked by before Dusty spoke. "What's up between you and my brother?"

Heat suffused her face, and she stared out the side window until her body temperature returned to normal. "Which brother?"

He chuckled. "Dexter."

"Nothing's going on between us."

"Why's he boarding the mustang at the Lazy S?"

"My father offered him the use of the corral because he doesn't have the cash to pay Dexter or the Cody ranch hands for helping with Lazy S cattle. And your mother wanted Zeus kept away from her horses. She's afraid the mustang might attack one of her stallions."

"Mom can be pretty persuasive, but are you positive Dexter isn't over at your ranch all the time because of you?"

"Exactly what are you getting at, Dusty? Dexter and I are friends. We were friends in high school and nothing's changed that." The thought of only *friendship* between her and Dexter the rest of their years made her sad.

"Dexter had a big ol' crush on you in high school."

"How come you never said anything to me?"

"'Cause I figured you'd dump me for him."

"Dump you?" She laughed. "You were the most popular boy in high school and every girl envied me. I wouldn't have given that up." Sadly, she spoke the truth.

She'd reveled in her popularity as Dusty's girlfriend. Curiosity got the best of her. "Did Dexter tell you he liked me back in high school?"

"No, but I caught him watching you all the time and I knew."

"And that didn't make you mad?"

"Nope. Dex was my brother. He'd never try to take what was mine." If only Dusty knew how true his words were.

Josie studied him out of the corner of her eye. Except for driving new vehicles, wearing a Cartier watch and the expensive hand-tooled leather cell phone case attached to his belt, no one would ever guess the cowboy was filthy rich. Today, he dressed in well-worn work clothes and—she glanced at the floor—scuffed-up cowboy boots.

"You're a schmuck, Dusty." Her declaration held no censure. "I was darn proud of myself for fending off your groping fingers as long as I did. If I hadn't been afraid of being replaced I probably wouldn't have slept with you."

Reflecting back on her high-school days, she acknowledged that she and Dusty had been typical teenagers. When Josie had made the decision to have sex with Dusty she'd had strong feelings for him, even though she'd never believed they'd marry. Dusty had been a young cowboy making a name for himself in rodeo, and she'd wanted to get out of Wyoming as fast as possible after graduation. A long-term commitment hadn't been in their future.

"Yeah, I had to work hard for that first kiss," Dusty said.

They laughed at the memory, then Josie asked, "How does it feel to be a father?"

"Guess I won't know until I meet Matt."

Regret pierced her conscience. If she'd been honest with Dusty from the get-go and told him he was going to be a father as soon as she'd discovered she was pregnant, they wouldn't be in this predicament right now.

If you'd told the truth four years ago, then the past three weeks with Dexter would never have happened.

Josie wanted to believe things had worked out the way they'd been meant to, but doubts lingered in her mind as Dusty turned into the long, winding driveway that led to J.W. and Anne Cody's spectacular home.

Chapter Eleven

Wow. Josie gaped when Dusty parked in front of the enormous home J.W. and Anne Cody had built for themselves.

"You know my father—" Dusty grinned "—nothing but the biggest and the best."

Her apartment in Santa Monica would fit inside the five-car garage. In any other setting the home would be obnoxiously ostentatious, but nestled among the spruce, fir and evergreen trees, the dark honey wood structure reminded her of a mountain lodge—for the rich and famous. "It's lovely," she said, admiring the diamond-shaped windows along the front of the home.

"Dad wanted enough bedrooms and bathrooms to entertain family and business acquaintances."

Track jumped out of the truck bed and chased after whatever scent tickled his nose, and Josie followed Dusty along the meandering stone walkway that led to the front door. The landscaping was beautiful—ornamental trees sprouted from a rock garden where red phlox flowed between strategically placed boulders. Clusters of lily of the valley with their delicate white bells sprouted from the garden and hummingbirds buzzed around the pink-flowering weigela shrubs that bordered the lush green grass.

"I hear water."

Dusty pointed to their left. "Mom had the landscaper divert some of the water from Cottonwood Creek to create a stream that runs through the backyard."

Josie deviated from the path to get a better look. Water spilled over several tiers of rock and green moss grew on the stones. Perched on the edge of a boulder sat a life-size cast-iron statue of a mermaid. Her hands were cupped around a butterfly the size of Josie's head, and water trickled over her giant fin.

"Hey, you coming?"

Josie retraced her steps and hurried after Dusty. He waited on the porch in front of the home's massive double-wide door with a leaded-glass transom.

When he reached for the door handle, she clutched his arm. "Wait."

"Nervous?" he asked.

She shook her head and motioned to the two-foot iron horse knocker. "Can I?"

He shrugged. "Go ahead."

The knocker weighed at least three pounds. She lifted the horse by its tail, then dropped it back into place. The thundering boom echoed off the mountain.

Dusty didn't wait for a housekeeper or a butler to open the door. She followed him inside, then froze, her eyes widening.

"Most people have that reaction when they see it for the first time."

If she thought the mermaid and the horse knocker were impressive, they were nothing compared to the monstrous bronze statue of a cowboy on a bucking horse that graced the foyer. J.W. might be worth millions in cattle, natural gas and horseflesh but his passion was definitely rodeo.

No wonder he hates my father.

It must have cut J.W. deeply that he'd been stuck in the shadows of Hank Charles. Had the Cody siblings loved the sport as much as their father or was J.W. living vicariously through his offspring, hoping they'd achieve a level of success he'd never attained?

"I called ahead and told Mom and Dad we'd be here by ten." Dusty checked his watch. "We're a little early. Let's wait in the office." He crossed the foyer and opened a set of French doors.

J.W.'s office was elegant yet inviting. A stone fireplace climbed the middle of one wall. Two custom wingback leather chairs faced the fireplace and floor-to-ceiling windows offered a view of the winding road leading to the house. J.W. would spot his visitors well before they parked in the driveway.

The large Western-style desk sported cowhide-studded leather panels and a cowboy on a bucking horse carved into the wooden panel at the front. A matching cowhide leather executive chair sat behind the desk. Gracing the top of the desk were a standard computer, leather blotter, hand-carved cigar box—*no doubt stuffed full of Cuban cigars*—cowboy statues that served as bookends for a handful of Zane Grey novels and an antique leather journal she suspected had once belonged to J.W.'s father.

Bookcases graced the walls on either side of the French doors. Rodeo trophies filled the shelves. She wandered closer and read the names engraved in the hardware: Walker, Jesse, Dusty, Dexter and Ellen. Even Anne had a few horse-breeding trophies in her name. No John Walker Cody. Had the Cody patriarch been so ashamed of his second-place finishes that he'd gotten rid of all his awards?

"Care for a drink?" Dusty motioned to the wet bar in the corner.

"No, thanks." She appreciated his attempt to play host, but frankly she wanted this meeting over with— yesterday. She sat opposite the desk on the camelback couch beneath the flat-panel TV hanging on the wall. "When was that taken?" She pointed to the family portrait above the fireplace mantel. Instead of a formal sitting, the Codys, wearing ranch attire, gathered in front of a split-rail fence somewhere on the property.

"Six years ago before Walker went into the Marines."

Fresh out of college, Walker sat next to his older brother, Jesse, on the top rail, behind J.W. and Anne, who stood in the center of the group. Still in college, Dusty and Dex squatted on the ground in front of their parents, and nineteen-year-old Ellen sat with arms around bent knees in front of the twins.

Pride and love shone from J.W.'s and Anne's eyes. As much as Josie worried they'd try to run roughshod over her, deep down she believed in her gut that the older couple loved their children with every inch of their being and that love would naturally extend to Matt.

The sound of a throat clearing preceded J.W. into the room. For a man who walked with a pronounced limp and a cane, J.W. made an intimidating figure. Strands of silver threaded his still-dark hair and he appeared much younger than his seventy years. He wore a designer Western shirt, black dress slacks, and his freshly oiled ostrich-skin boots winked beneath the recessed lights.

The Cody patriarch fidgeted before sitting in the desk chair. He was nervous. Good. That leveled the playing field—a little.

"Josie." Age hadn't weakened the baritone voice she recalled from her high school days and his eyes flashed with the same steely glint. "Hello, Mr. Cody."

"Where's Mom?" Dusty asked.

"On her way." J.W. struck up a conversation with Dusty, pointedly ignoring Josie. "I hope you plan to prepare for the Hoedown on Saturday."

"Yeah, I'm sticking around."

"Dexter practiced once with Ricky," J.W. said. "That was a disaster."

"Has Digger's leg healed?"

"I'm not worried about the horse. I'm worried about your brother." J.W.'s gaze shifted to Josie. "Dexter's been distracted lately."

Josie was no longer a seventeen-year-old afraid to stand up to the big-bad father of her boyfriend. "Dexter and my dad struck a fair deal, Mr. Cody. Dexter's help with the cattle in exchange for boarding the mustang at the Lazy S."

"My son has no business messing around with wild horses."

She glanced at Dusty, expecting him to jump to his brother's defense, but he chose to stare out the window instead.

"Josie, what a nice surprise. Why, it's been years since I've seen you." Flashing a warm smile, Anne Cody walked to her husband's side, her silver bob brushing against her jaw. She stood by J.W.'s chair, one hand resting on his shoulder, a stunning three-carat marquise diamond winking from her ring finger. "I hope your father's recovery is going well."

At least she'd asked about their neighbor, unlike J.W. "Dad's much better. Mom's having trouble keeping him from overdoing." Silence ensued, and Josie felt compelled to speak. "How was your trip to the Black Rock Ranch?"

"Wonderful. They breed such magnificent horses." Anne paused when Dusty left his post by the window and joined Josie on the couch. "I picked out a new mare for Mr. Lucky Son," Anne continued. "The foal or colt will go to our first grandson, Clay."

Oh, dear. Wait until Anne and J.W. learned they'd already had a grandson these past four years—their first biological grandchild.

J.W. cleared his throat. "What's this meeting about, Dusty?"

Dusty knew best how to handle his parents, so Josie remained silent. "I have some news to share."

"You two aren't getting back together, are you?" J.W. wasn't going to make this easy.

"Dear, let Dusty speak." Anne offered Josie an apologetic smile.

"Mom…Dad…" Dusty sucked in a huge breath, the air rushing out with his words. "Josie and I have a son together. His name's Matt."

Anne's hand went to her chest and her face drained of color. Clutching the edge of the desk, she stared into space.

The only sounds were Anne's labored breathing and the ticking wall clock. After several seconds, Anne's dazed expression transformed into a frown. "Dusty, shame on you for keeping your child a secret from us. Why in the world didn't you tell us you'd gotten Josie pregnant?"

Before Josie had a chance to defend Dusty, Anne asked, "Where is my grandson? When can I see him?"

"Hold up, Mom."

Josie peeked at J.W. She wished she hadn't. If his reddish-purple skin tone was any indication, his head was about to implode. "You two have a lot of explaining to do."

"Matt is four years old," Dusty said.

The hand on Anne's chest moved to her throat. She looked as if someone had thrown a noose around her neck and pulled it taut. Josie ached for the hurt she'd caused the older woman.

"You've kept our grandson a secret for four years?" J.W. bellowed at his son.

Dusty didn't deserve his father's outrage. Josie had made the decision to keep Matt a secret. She had to face the music. "Dusty wasn't aware Matt even existed until a few weeks ago when I returned to Markton."

"Are you certain the child is yours, Dusty?" J.W. asked.

Josie didn't flinch at the implied insult—she'd expected as much from a man like J.W.

"Josie says he's got my dimple." Dusty grinned.

Anne's eyes widened. "You haven't met your son?"

"Not yet," Dusty said.

"This is terrible." Anne sank into the chair in front of the fireplace and held her face in her hands.

"We had a right to know our grandson existed. Why did you keep him a secret?" J.W. glared at Josie.

"I had my reasons." Had the codger forgotten he'd swindled her father? A stare-down ensued.

J.W. backed off first. "What's done is done. The important thing is you two get married and make my grandson an official Cody."

"I've already proposed."

Dusty called "I think we should get married" a proposal?

"Josie wants time to think about it," Dusty said.

Chicken. "What Dusty means is that I turned down his proposal."

Anne's head snapped up and she gasped.

"Any woman in her right mind would marry a Cody in a heartbeat." J.W. leaned across his desk as if his intimidating posture would persuade her to see things his way.

If Josie wasn't so frustrated with how the meeting was playing out she might have found J.W.'s bafflement comical. She suspected few women would turn their nose up at a life of luxury.

"I'm sure Josie will reconsider once she understands it's in Matt's best interest to carry the Cody name." Anne stood. "I'll need at least a month to plan the wedding."

Wedding? Josie attempted to give Dusty the evil eye but he was busy studying the worn-down heel on his boot.

"We'll have it here at the house by the pool," Anne continued. "What's your favorite color, Josie? I'll need to know when I speak with the florist."

"Let's hold off on any wedding plans." Josie took a deep breath. "I haven't yet told my parents that Dusty is Matt's father."

J.W. rubbed his brow but remained silent—for a change.

"The best thing to do right now is nothing." Her statement earned another scowl from J.W. Josie kept a straight face but her insides chuckled. Who would have thought taunting Wyoming's cattle and gas baron would be such fun? "We all need time to let this news sink in before any decisions about the future are made."

"Sounds good." Dusty motioned to the door, and Josie jumped at the chance to escape.

"Wait!" Anne cried. "When can we see our grandson?"

"I think Dusty should meet Matt first before he's introduced to the rest of the family," Josie said.

"Give me a little time—" Dusty stared at the tips of his boots "—to get used to the idea of being a father."

"You'd better become used to being a father and a husband." J.W. dared Josie to protest.

Not caring if Dusty followed her, Josie made a beeline for the front door.

"Hold up." Dusty took the porch steps two at a time. "I'm sorry my dad lost his temper. He doesn't like surprises."

Obviously. Josie hopped into Dusty's truck. She wanted to get home and hug her son. Now that the confrontation with J.W. and Anne was over, reality had sunk in. The world she and Matt knew would never be the same. Until now, she'd been in control of her son's life—the sole decision maker. No longer. Dusty would have a say, and Josie knew Anne and J.W. would try to influence their son's *say*.

Dusty stuck his fingers into his mouth and whistled. Track bounded from the woods and jumped into the truck bed, tail wagging. Halfway down the mountain road, Dusty broke the silence. "You're going to reconsider my marriage proposal, aren't you?"

Back to that again? "Let's be brutally honest, Dusty. You don't want to marry me for Matt's sake or to defend my honor or even to keep the Markton tongues from wagging. The only reason you proposed in the first place is because you knew your father would insist."

He allowed her comment to slide—only because she'd nailed the truth. They settled into a companionable silence, and Josie's thoughts strayed to Dexter. She missed him. Missed his smile. Missed the way he stared at her out of the corner of his eye when he didn't think she noticed. Missed the way he tilted his head while she talked—as if carefully considering each word she spoke.

She never had to guess if she had Dexter's attention. His every action proved his awareness of her. He'd made her believe she was the center of his world—*until Dusty had returned from Canada*. Now Dexter acted as if he couldn't get far enough away from her.

Dusty parked in front of the Lazy S ranch house, and Josie's attention shifted to the corral by the barn. Had she been so uptight this morning that she hadn't observed the horse trailer hitched to Dexter's truck? Was he taking the mustang back to the Cottonwood Ranch?

The front door opened and Matt ran out of the house. He waved at her as he raced past the truck. "Mr. D, Mr. D!" he called, heading toward the corral.

Dusty watched his son and his brother engage in conversation. "Matt's become attached to Dexter." The statement held no censure. No jealousy. No anger. Just fact.

"Yes." Matt found his male role model. Dexter walked on water. Roped the moon. Sailed the Seven Seas. And broke hearts—hers.

"That's good," Dusty said. "Dexter's solid."

Too mentally exhausted to decipher the meaning behind Dusty's comment, Josie asked, "Would you like to meet Matt?"

Dusty tapped the steering wheel with his fingertips. Shifted in his seat. Glanced in the rearview mirror. The poor man was a wreck.

"If you're not ready, that's okay." She'd rather he be relaxed when he spoke to Matt for the first time.

"Yeah." Dusty's shoulders sagged. "I'll wait."

Josie sympathized with Dusty—he hadn't asked to be put in this position. Her gaze shifted to Dexter standing in the corral by Zeus. She smiled.

"What are you grinning at?"

She pointed to the corral. "Dex finally got Zeus to accept a saddle."

Dusty watched his brother for a minute, then said, "Why don't you discuss my proposal with your parents and see what they think."

"It doesn't matter what anyone thinks." *Except Dexter.* "I refuse to give up my job and move Matt away from his friends." The only person who could change her mind was Dexter. She hopped out of the truck and shut the door. Before she had a chance to say goodbye Dusty sped off like a bat out of hell.

"Mr. D put a saddle on Zeus!" Matt shouted across the ranch yard.

Josie joined her two favorite cowboys by the corral.

"Mr. D's gonna ride Zeus, right Mr. D?"

"Eventually," Dexter said.

"I'm impressed."

A million questions swirled in Dexter's blue eyes.

"How did you manage to get the saddle on him?" she asked.

"Mr. D found out Zeus likes peppermints," Matt answered for Dexter.

"Really?"

Dexter smiled—not a full grin but a tiny curve of the lips. "Zeus ripped my shirt pocket trying to get at my Altoids tin."

"I'm gonna go tell Grandpa Zeus likes candy." Matt raced off, leaving Josie and Dexter alone.

He cleared his throat. "How'd they take the news?"

No need to ask who *they* were. "As well as any grandparents who just found out they had a grandchild."

"Why didn't Dusty stay and meet Matt?"

"He's not ready." The muscle along Dexter's jaw bunched, and Josie came to Dusty's defense. "Don't be too hard on your brother. He's still in shock over the whole fatherhood thing."

Dexter walked off, leaving Josie the choice to follow or not. She trailed him inside the barn, where he stopped to fill a bucket with grain.

A warm tingling sensation raced across her skin at the memory of her and Dexter in another barn.... She closed her eyes and breathed deeply as intimate images filled her mind.

"You okay?"

"I don't know." Josie opened her eyes to find Dexter standing a foot away. "We need to talk about what happened."

"Yesterday was a mistake, Josie."

His cold words pierced her heart like a pitchfork. "So that's it? Almost making love to me meant nothing to you?"

"No!" His chest heaved, giving Josie hope that their intimate encounter had affected him as deeply as it had her. "We're in an impossible situation." Each word sounded as if it had been pulled straight from the bottom of his gut.

"I wouldn't say impossible."

"Matt is Dusty's son, not mine."

"What difference does that make for us?"

"It makes a hell of a difference. Dusty has a right to come first in Matt's life."

"No one's denying Dusty the opportunity to be a father."

"Matt deserves a real family and you and Dusty deserve a chance to have a meaningful relationship."

Panic gripped Josie's stomach and twisted painfully. "What are you saying?"

"Maybe I'm old-fashioned, but I think you should marry Dusty."

"You want me to marry your brother after we... after we almost..." She couldn't finish the sentence, because the idea was ludicrous. She wasn't sure what hurt more—that Dexter was so damned honorable or that he didn't love her enough to fight for her.

"I don't love your brother." She held up a hand. "And don't tell me I might learn to love Dusty eventually." How could she, when her heart was so full of Dexter?

"Josie." He stubbed his toe against the drain cover on the cement floor.

"Dex." She cursed the catch in her voice.

His eyes glistened with pain.

Don't. Don't say it, Dex. Please, don't say it.

"It's best we put our feelings for each other aside and move on."

The breath whooshed from her lungs in a giant gust of wind, leaving her dazed.

"I'm taking Zeus with me when I leave today. Now that Dusty's back he can help your father around the ranch."

If Dexter wasn't going to fight for her…them…then relocating to Wyoming was out of the question.

Fighting back tears, she held her head high as she walked out of the barn. Had she known her decision to keep Matt a secret would lead to such heartbreak she'd have come forward as soon as she'd found out she was pregnant—the feud between J.W. and her father be damned.

What's done is done.

The only path left to take was the one in front of her.

Chapter Twelve

"Zeus suits him. Think I'll keep the name." Bud Masterson stood next to Dexter outside the round pen. "The rumors about you were dead-on, Cody."

"Rumors?" Dexter had been in a foul mood since Dusty had returned from Canada. As soon as Masterson left with the mustang, Dexter planned to find a dark hole to crawl into and lick his wounds. He couldn't believe he'd lied to Josie—insisting that almost making love had been a mistake. The truth was the bull ride with her had been the best and the worst thing he'd ever done.

"Folks claim you never break a horse's spirit," Masterson droned on.

Dexter might be good with horses but he sucked with women. He'd broken Josie's spirit yesterday even though he'd had her and Matt's best interests in mind. No wonder his heart felt as though it had been hacked to pieces by a meat cleaver.

Shoving his misery aside, Dexter focused on the mustang. "Every time you put a saddle on Zeus, take him for a long run."

"I'll make sure he gets plenty of exercise."

"Let Zeus choose the direction and don't pull back on the reins for the first two or three miles. He needs to believe he's in control. Once he tires, he'll cooperate and be less eager to escape."

"I'll do everything in my power to make sure Zeus believes he's calling the shots."

"Hey, Dex." Ricky stepped outside the barn. "J.W. wants you up at the office. Pronto."

Masterson handed Dexter a check. "Pleasure doing business with you."

Dexter clicked his tongue and the mustang lifted his head and stared. *You're as free as you'll ever be, Zeus. Make the best of the second chance you've been given.*

"Ricky will help you load him." Dexter signaled to the ranch hand, then walked to the office. Doris flashed a smile when he entered the building.

"Go right in, Dexter. Your father's waiting for you."

"Shut the door," J.W. commanded as soon as Dexter waltzed into the room.

Closed doors in the Cody family meant one thing— an argument hovered on the horizon. "What's up?"

"This isn't public knowledge yet, so keep what I'm about to tell you under your hat." He cleared his throat. "Your brother Dusty is a father."

"I know. The resemblance between Dusty and Matt is difficult to miss."

"You know about my grandson?" J.W.'s voice thundered through the room.

"I ran into Josie and Matt at the Sweetwater County Fair in Lander at the beginning of the month. Josie and Dusty asked me to keep their secret until Dusty returned from his movie shoot in Canada."

"Since when do the Codys keep secrets from each other?" Clearly J.W. didn't appreciate being in the dark.

Hoping to move the conversation along, Dexter said, "Is that all you wanted to tell me?"

"No. I need your help. Actually your brother needs your help."

"Which brother?"

"Don't be a smart-ass. Dusty claims Josie Charles refuses to marry him and do what's right by my grandson."

Relief zapped the strength from Dexter's legs, and he sank into the chair in front of the desk. He'd prayed to God, asking Him to do what was best for Matt, Josie and Dusty, which Dexter believed meant Josie and Dusty had to give marriage a try. Then he'd prayed to the Devil, asking the horned villain to make Josie stand firm and refuse to marry Dusty, because deep down Dexter believed she belonged to *him*.

Evidently the Devil had won the first round. "Josie's an adult. She can choose to marry who she wants."

"She lost that right when she gave birth to a Cody."

Dexter hadn't seen his father this upset since he'd overheard his parents arguing months ago about that old rumor that had resurfaced, claiming J.W. had had an affair shortly after he'd married Dexter's mother and the affair had resulted in a child being born. Dexter figured the loose tongue had belonged to someone who'd held a grudge against the Codys—and there were plenty of folks who envied the powerful Wyoming family.

"Don't take this the wrong way, Dad, but you're sticking your nose into something that's none of your business."

"I have a grandson who deserves to bear the Cody name. Come hell or high water that child is going to claim his rightful place in this family."

If Dexter had any doubts about his father's loyalty toward his mother he could put them to rest. J.W.'s insistence that Matt bear the Cody name confirmed that his father would never have permitted one of his own offspring—even an illegitimate one—to go unacknowledged. Family meant everything to J.W.

"How am I supposed to help Josie and Dusty?" Dexter asked.

"Your job is to hound Dusty until he convinces Josie to marry him."

What the hell? Frustrated, Dexter lashed out. "I'm surprised you'd even want Josie to be part of the family."

"What are you talking about?"

"You hate Hank Charles's guts."

"*Hate*'s an awful strong word." He cleared his throat. "We have our reasons for distrusting one another."

"How come you won't admit there's more than rodeo buckles standing between you and Hank?"

"It's none of your business, son."

Hating that his father refused to be truthful with him, Dexter stood. "And what happens between Dusty and Josie is none of my business, either."

"You're the only one who's ever been able to talk sense into Dusty."

Not true. Dusty had a mind of his own. If he didn't want to listen to reason—he didn't. Running off to Canada when he should have stayed and worked things out with Josie had been evidence of that.

"I'm not asking you, Dexter. I'm telling you—help Dusty find a way to persuade Josie to marry him." J.W. shook his head. "Would have been easier on the family if you'd gotten Josie pregnant. You're the responsible one. You'd do the right thing in a heartbeat and wouldn't second-guess your decision."

Second-guess your decision…

The words haunted Dexter. Having to step aside so Dusty could claim Josie for his own—a second time—made him physically ill. Feeling the walls close in on him, he sprang from the chair. "I'll see what I can do." He stormed out of the office, ignoring Doris's smile.

By the time Dexter arrived at the practice ring he was good and ready to pick a fight with his twin. He entered the ring and walked straight up to Dusty, who was grooming his horse, Uno. "Where the hell have you been?"

"Right here waiting for your sorry butt." Dusty flashed his trademark grin.

That did it. Dexter had had enough of his brother's cocky attitude. He hauled off and punched Dusty in the jaw. His brother stumbled backward, tripping over his feet. Spooked, Uno trotted to the other side of the enclosure.

"God damn it, Dex." Dusty rubbed his jaw. "What's gotten into you?"

"You want to know why I'm pissed?" Dexter loomed over his brother's sprawled body. "Because Dad's given me the chore of talking sense into you and Josie."

"What?" Dusty crawled to his knees.

Dexter placed a boot in the middle of his brother's chest and shoved him backward. "I'm tired of your bullshit." Dexter ignored the crowd of ranch hands gathering to watch the spectacle. "Stand up," he commanded.

"Why? So you can hit me again?"

"Yes."

"Jeez, Dex, give me a break." Dusty dabbed at a drop of blood that oozed from his cracked lip.

A feeling of helplessness fueled Dexter's anger, and he grabbed his brother by the shirt collar and hauled him to his feet. Before he had a chance to wind up and punch him again, Dusty kicked Dexter's feet out from under him and he fell forward, taking Dusty down with him. Grunts and groans ensued as they scuffled in the dirt. Dexter ended up on top. "When are you gonna grow up?"

"You're the one who's acting like a sissy." Dusty landed a punch to Dexter's breadbasket, knocking the wind from him.

"I'm tired…of cleaning up…your…messes," Dexter wheezed. Dusty pushed Dexter onto his back and straddled his brother. He opened his mouth to speak, but Dexter bucked him right over his head. Dusty sprawled face-first on the ground.

The ranch hands shouted bets on which twin would win. Dusty was a better fighter and had won most of the scuffles they'd gotten into when they'd been younger. But right now Dexter was fired up enough to have the edge.

Dexter struggled to his knees first, then his feet, but before he took a step, Dusty grabbed his boot heel and Dexter hit the ground again.

"Mind tellin' me what the hell we're fighting about?" Dusty said.

"Josie, you damned fool. Who else do you think this is about?" Dexter took a swing, but his punch landed on Dusty's shoulder instead of his face.

"What about Josie?" Dusty crawled on his hands and knees but didn't get far before Dexter gripped the belt loop on his jeans and tugged hard. The material ripped.

"Hey! Watch the clothes!"

Chest heaving, Dexter said, "Do you know how lucky you are to have a son as great as Matt?" A hush fell over the ranch hands. Dexter didn't care if the whole frickin' world knew Dusty had fathered a child out of wedlock. "And you'll find no better woman than Josie for a wife."

Hanging on to each other for balance, the brothers struggled to their feet. "You know what I think?" Dusty spat at the ground. "You're in love with Josie and you wish Matt was your kid."

The accusation pierced Dexter's heart, and he punched his finger into Dusty's chest. "What would you know about love?" Another shove. "You go through women faster than a six-pack of beer."

"You've had a crush on Josie since high school. You're just miffed she chose me."

"Some choice. You won't even stand up for what's right."

"The hell you say!" Dusty locked arms with Dexter, and the brothers crashed to the dirt. They rolled from side to side, kicking up a cloud of dust.

"If you're so concerned about Josie why don't you marry her?" Dusty landed another punch and stars danced before Dexter's eyes.

"You're Matt's father and that boy deserves a real family." Dexter pushed away from Dusty. "For once in your life take responsibility for your actions."

"I wish to hell everyone would quit telling me that."

Dexter sat up. "Maybe if you put others before yourself—"

Dusty socked Dexter in the arm.

Dexter winced. "Watch the roping arm, you ass."

"Sorry. You okay?" When Dexter didn't answer, Dusty turned his shoulder toward Dexter. "Here. Punch me back."

Dexter punched Dusty's arm, but not hard. They wouldn't have a chance in hell of winning Saturday if Dusty's arm was too bruised to throw a rope.

They sat in the dirt for several seconds, both gasping for breath. Then Dusty confessed, "I'm frickin' scared, Dex. Okay? There, I said it. I'm scared."

"Of what?"

"I want to be Matt's father but I don't know how. What if I screw up? What if the kid hates my guts? Huh? What then?"

Sympathy for his twin cooled Dexter's anger. Dusty was a winner—he'd always been a winner. The thought of losing scared the bejesus out of him. Dexter wished like hell he could take Dusty's place, but their father would accept nothing less than Dusty marrying Josie. "You have to try, Dusty. You can't quit on Matt or Josie."

"What about you?" Dusty said.

"What about me?"

"You have feelings for Josie."

Dexter opened his mouth, then snapped it closed. What was the use? Anything he said would be a lie. "Never mind me," Dexter grumbled. "But I swear to you on Grandpa's grave if you mistreat Josie or make her regret marrying you I'll—"

Dusty elbowed Dexter in the gut. "You'll what? Beat me?"

"What the hell's going on!" Big brother Jesse entered the practice ring and strode toward the twins.

"Get lost, Jesse." Dusty climbed to his feet, then offered Dexter a hand.

"This is between me and Dusty." Dexter stared defiantly at their older brother.

"You made it my business when you attracted all this attention." Jesse swept his arm out in front of him. "Instead of working, the ranch hands are watching you two dummies make fools of yourselves." Jesse whipped his white hat off and pointed it at his brothers. "Keep it up and Dad'll come out here and tear into your asses."

Too exhausted to argue, Dexter looked at Dusty and they read each other's minds. A moment later they both hauled off and socked Jesse in the gut. Their big brother's favorite cowboy hat fell to the ground, and he clutched his stomach. Bug-eyed, Jesse opened and closed his mouth, but no sound escaped.

"That's for sticking your nose where it doesn't belong," Dusty said.

"Hey, who won?" Ricky shouted as Dexter and Dusty staggered together out of the practice ring.

"Dusty!" Paco shouted.

"No way! Dexter got the last punch in," Slim countered.

The cheering stopped when Dexter and Dusty stumbled into their father.

"What's going on?" J.W. boomed.

"Dexter and I had a little disagreement," Dusty said.

J.W. motioned to their torn clothes and bloodied lips, then directed his words to Dexter. "This is how you planned to coax your brother into convincing Josie Charles to marry him—by beating him up?"

Dusty scowled at Dexter. "Back to being Dad's little do-gooder."

Dexter cocked his arm but his father intercepted the punch with his hand. "How do you expect to win on Saturday if neither of you can throw a rope?"

Good ol' Dad. Rodeo always came first.

Dusty shuffled off to his apartment above the barn, and Dexter returned to the house. He had a phone call to make—one he'd rather not.

DEXTER HEARD THE TRUCK STOP at the other end of the bridge, but he kept his back to the road. He'd called Josie shortly after his fight with Dusty and asked if she'd meet him at the Wallaghany Bridge fifteen miles east of Markton.

Every teenager within a fifty-mile radius of Markton knew about the walking bridge suspended over the

Wallaghany River. The spot was popular with high-school students who used the bridge as a diving board into the river below. Dexter remembered one particular summer afternoon when he'd tagged along with Josie and Dusty. Man-oh-man, had Josie looked hot in her smokin' red bikini.

Josie's boots clunked against the wooden planks. She stopped a few feet away. "You're not thinking of jumping, are you?"

He'd given it a thought or two but decided he didn't care to stink like fish. He faced Josie, bracing himself for her reaction.

She gasped. "What happened to your face?" She lurched forward, but Dexter stepped out of reach. Her touch would have been too painful. Seeing her pretty face and knowing what he had to say was torture enough.

Eyes wide with hurt, she lowered her arm to her side.

"Dusty and I got into a scuffle."

A moist film covered her pretty brown eyes, and he yearned to haul Josie into his arms and hug her. He wanted to rub his nose in her hair and smell her sweet-scented shampoo. Feel her body pressed to his.

He just flat-out wanted her.

"Your fight had to do with me," Josie said.

"Dusty wants to do right by you." The words damn near choked him.

"I don't love Dusty. We'd never be happy."

His father's words echoed through Dexter's brain.... *Would have been a hell of a lot easier on the family if you'd gotten Josie pregnant. You're the responsible one. You'd do the right thing in a heartbeat and wouldn't second-guess your decision.* "If you give Dusty half a chance you two might be happy. And Matt deserves a mother and a father who live together."

"You're not much of a fighter, are you?"

Dexter rubbed his battered jaw. "I gave as good as I got."

"That's not what I meant and you know it. You're not a fighter...you're a quitter."

Did Josie have any idea how difficult it was for him to step aside in order to give Matt, her and his brother the chance to be a real family? His throat closed, and the words he wanted to say in his defense went unsaid.

"I believed the time we spent together the past few weeks meant something to you." She shook her head. "But I can't compete against your high moral code. I don't know that anyone can."

When she turned to leave, he found his voice. "Tomorrow, Dusty's dropping by the Lazy S to meet Matt."

"Fine. We'll be there."

Josie crossed the bridge and hopped into her father's truck. She hit the gas hard and the tires spun before gaining traction and sending the truck lurching down the dirt road.

Chapter Thirteen

"I have something to tell you," Josie said when she stepped into her parents' kitchen. After meeting with Dexter on the Wallaghany Bridge, she'd driven around for an hour until her temper had cooled. One minute she loved Dexter to distraction—the next she wanted to clobber him over the head with an iron skillet. "Maybe you should sit down."

Her parents exchanged worried glances. "Bad news?" her mother asked.

"No." At least she hoped not. Josie had imagined this moment for years. Now that the time had come to divulge the identity of her son's father she had mixed feelings—the biggest of which was fear. Fear of how her father would react. Her main reason for keeping Dusty's identity a secret had been her father's animosity toward J.W. Josie worried that Matt would become the pawn of a tug-of-war match between the two families.

"Where's Matt?" Josie didn't want her son to overhear the conversation.

"Outside on the tire swing." Her father chuckled. "That rascal's been running wild all day."

Josie worried Matt would miss the freedom of his grandfather's ranch after they returned to California, where Matt would have to attend day care eight hours a day while she worked.

Her father rapped his knuckles against the table. "What's on your mind, daughter?"

"I want you to know who Matt's father is."

"We've known all along, dear," her mother said.

The breath in Josie's lungs evaporated. "But—"

"Two months after you mentioned Dusty passed through L.A. and stayed at your apartment, you turned up pregnant," her father said. "Wasn't hard to figure out he was the father."

"And when Matt celebrated his first birthday—" her mother spoke "—we noticed the dimple in his right cheek—just like his daddy's."

"Why didn't you say something then?" Josie asked.

"I wanted to tell you our suspicions, but…" Her mother stared pointedly at her father.

"I figured J.W. would make life miserable for you and Matt," her father admitted.

"Me, too." Josie rubbed her brow, pressing her thumbs against the pounding pulse in her temples.

Her father cleared his throat. "I shouldn't have told you about J.W. swindling me out of those gas wells. Who knows, maybe you and Dusty would have gotten together and—"

"No, Dad. After Dusty's visit, I realized that what I felt for him wasn't love." She shrugged. "I don't believe I ever loved Dusty. I was enamored with his popularity and enjoyed sharing the spotlight with him in high school."

"I have a confession to make, also," her mother said. Josie doubted her mother would ever do anything that needed forgiving.

"I went along with your father's insistence that we keep our suspicions to ourselves because I was afraid Anne Cody would buy our grandson's love and lavish him with expensive gifts that your father and I couldn't afford to give Matt."

Josie hugged her mother. "This is my wrongdoing, not yours."

"What are you and Dusty planning to do?" her father asked.

"Dusty proposed."

Her mother frowned. "But I thought you two didn't love—"

"We don't. J.W. is insisting we marry."

"That no-good wisecracker can't make my daughter—"

"Dad, calm down, or you'll mess up your heart again." Good grief, another attack might be fatal.

"What about Dexter? You love him, don't you?"

She should have expected her mother would guess her feelings for Dexter. "Yes. But he insists that the right thing for everyone involved is for me and Dusty to marry."

"I've seen the way Dexter looks at you," her father said. "He's a love-struck fool."

"Doesn't make any sense." Josie's mother left the table and prepared a pot of coffee. "Why would Dexter want you to marry his brother when he loves you?"

Throat tight, Josie whispered, "He believes Matt, Dusty and I deserve a chance to be a real family."

"Men." Her mother grumbled an unintelligible word.

Josie jumped to Dexter's defense. "He wants what's best for Matt and me." Josie both hated and loved Dexter for his decency. "J.W. underestimated me, because I'll never agree to marry Dusty."

Her father grinned. "That's my girl."

"Hank, stop it." Her mother returned to the table. "Have you told Dexter how you feel about him?"

A cold chill rushed through Josie. Had she said the words to Dexter? Had she told him she loved him—or just that she didn't love Dusty? "Um…"

"Josie," her mother said, "if you're not marrying Dusty or Dexter, what are your plans for the future?"

Matt loved the ranch, and she hated to make him move back to California. But the idea of living in the same town as the man she loved but couldn't be with was more than she could handle.

"You know we'd love for you and Matt to stay here," her mother said when Josie remained silent. "Any chance you could find work in Markton or Cody?"

"Possibly." Josie was certain her employer would help her obtain freelance projects for a doctor's or lawyer's office, but she didn't want to get her parents' hopes up.

"I vote you and Matt move back home. I like having my grandson around," her father said.

In many ways life would be easier if she lived in Markton or nearby. There would be no custody battle over Matt. Her son would have lots of uncles and an aunt to lavish attention on him. Both sets of grandparents would have an opportunity to spend as much time with their grandson as they wished. With her father's serious heart condition, every day Matt was able to spend with his grandpa Charles was a blessing.

If nothing else, Josie considered the move for purely selfish reasons. She hoped that if Matt grew up around family he'd forgive her for keeping him from Dusty the first four years of his life.

Josie glanced at her father. "How do you feel about sharing your grandson with J.W.?"

"I got a head start at being the favorite grandpa. I'll just have to work hard to keep it that way."

Her mother frowned. "What are you going to do about Dexter?"

"Nothing."

"But—"

"The Codys have a strong sense of responsibility toward family. Dexter won't budge on this." Josie wondered how many days, weeks and months would go by before her heart stopped hoping he'd change his mind about her.

"What time should we expect Dusty tomorrow?" her mother asked.

"Around noon. I'll tell Matt before Dusty arrives." Her son was a resilient kid, and he'd weather this latest change in his life with the same enthusiasm he showed in everything he did.

All talked out, she left the table, then paused in the kitchen doorway. "Mom, Dad...thanks for..." Her throat swelled shut.

"We love you, dear. Whatever happens...whatever you decide about the future, we're here for you."

JOSIE WAS STANDING SENTRY at the front window when she observed the Cottonwood Ranch truck turn onto the gravel road leading to her parents' house.

The day of reckoning had arrived.

She'd broken the news to Matt over breakfast that his father was coming to see him. At first her son had stared as if he'd misunderstood her. Then he'd said, "Is he gonna quit traveling?"

His question had broken her heart. For so long Matt had bought into the lie that his father traveled and didn't have time to spend with him.

"Matt, your dad's here," Josie hollered down the hallway. Matt bolted from his bedroom and ran past her out the front door. Her parents stood in the kitchen doorway, their wrinkled faces full of worry and love.

Josie flashed a smile, hoping to reassure them.

"We'll be right here if you need us." Her father hugged her.

Taking a deep breath, she joined Matt on the front porch. As the truck drew nearer, Josie saw that Dexter sat behind the wheel. Her heart soared. Had he changed his mind? Had he come along with Dusty to insist she marry him instead of his brother?

Her hopes were dashed when Dexter parked the truck but remained inside the vehicle as Dusty got out. She couldn't read his expression behind the tinted windshield, but she guessed he wasn't smiling.

Dusty walked toward the porch.

Matt tugged on her shirtsleeve. "He looks just like Mr. D, Mom."

Dusty stopped at the bottom step and removed his hat. Dexter hadn't lied yesterday—he'd given as good as he'd gotten during the scuffle with his brother.

"You look like Mr. D," Matt said.

"That's because we're brothers."

Dusty attempted a smile—not an easy task with a split lip.

Matt descended two steps until he stood eye to eye with Dusty. "What happened to your face?"

"Mr. D and I were practicing for a rodeo and the cow gave us a bit of trouble," Dusty lied.

"Are you really my dad?"

"Yes, I am, Matt."

Josie held her breath.

"Mom said you couldn't be my dad 'cause you travel a lot. Where did you travel?"

"All over the country. I compete in a lot of rodeos."

"How come you didn't want me and Mom to come with you?"

Josie opened her mouth to field the question, but Dusty beat her to it. "Your mom had to work, and rodeos are dangerous places for little kids."

Josie didn't deserve Dusty's gracious explanation and swore right then she'd never interfere with Dusty and Matt's relationship.

"Oh." Matt shuffled his boots against the step and continued to glance at Dexter in the truck, as if he needed reassurance from Mr. D.

"I'm not a little kid anymore." Matt looked at Josie. "Right, Mom?"

"You're not as little but you're still a kid."

"Mr. D. says I can be a cowboy when I grow up."

"You'll make a fine cowboy someday," Dusty said.

Out of the corner of her eye, Josie saw the driver's-side door open and Dexter step out. Her heart ached at the tense lines bracketing his mouth. She wanted to demand he fight for Matt's affections. Fight for the right to be his father, too. Fight to make her and Matt and him a family. *Blasted cowboy.* Why did Dexter have to play the hero? For once why couldn't he take what *he* wanted and to hell with everyone else?

"Are you gonna live at my house?" Matt asked.

Josie intervened. "Honey, we'll iron out the details later. Right now I think your father would like to get to know you a little better."

"Okay. I like soccer and Grandma's chocolate cake. Mr. D taught me to ride a horse. Right, Mr. D?" Matt shouted in Dexter's direction.

"That's right. Maybe your father can take you riding one of these days."

"Wanna see the horse Mr. D lets me ride?" Matt asked Dusty.

"Sure." Dusty held out his hand, and Matt didn't think twice before clasping his father's fingers and leading the way to the barn.

Left alone with Dexter, Josie fidgeted. An uncomfortable silence ensued until he spoke. "Is your father around?"

"He's inside."

"I need to speak with him."

That's it? Dexter wanted to talk to her father but had nothing to say to her? Angry and hurt she retreated inside the house and almost plowed her father over. "Eavesdropping?"

"Just making sure everyone behaves."

"Dexter wants to talk to you." Josie ignored her mother's questioning look and fled down the hallway. She slammed the bedroom door behind her, then burst into tears.

"HANK." DEXTER GREETED the old man when he stepped onto the porch.

"Take a load off." Hank sat in one of two rockers on the porch.

If Josie's father had known what Dexter intended to show him, he might not have been so neighborly. Dexter climbed the steps and sat in the other rocker.

"Whatcha got there?" Hank motioned to the surveys in Dexter's hand.

"My brother, Walker, discovered these at our grandfather's cabin on Carter Mountain." Dexter cleared his throat. "Looks like more than a few buckles stand between you and my father."

"What are you saying, son?"

"Walker found a copy of the survey you had done on your property before you sold it to my father. He compared it to the survey my father had commissioned. I'm sure you're well aware the results were contradictory."

Hank stared into space as if his mind had wandered back in time.

"I'm guessing one of the reasons Josie refused to return to Markton after Matt had been born was because she believed my father had swindled you out of a lot of money when he paid you a third of what your land was worth."

"I've done some things I'm not proud of—one of 'em being I lied to my daughter. I knew Dusty fathered Matt, but I worried that if J.W. knew about Matt he'd take my grandchild away from my daughter."

Dexter's father would never have done that, but this wasn't the first time he'd heard of people afraid of the

Cody wealth and power. When Hank didn't elaborate, Dexter said, "I'd like to hear your side of the story. And then I intend to make things right."

"Ain't nothing to make right." Hank leveled a bleak-eyed stare on Dexter. "When Pennyton and his wife died and left me the Lazy S, their son challenged the will. I hired a lawyer and racked up a hefty stack of bills, but I kept the ranch. The following spring the herd got sick and I lost nearly every head. I was gonna lose the ranch if I didn't find a way to make some quick cash." Hank rubbed his knees. "Right after I'd inherited the Lazy S, J.W. had asked if I'd sell off six hundred acres to him. I refused."

A run of bad luck was enough to change a man's mind.

"I approached your father and asked if he was still interested in buying Lazy S land. He offered to pay to have the survey done, but I didn't trust him, so I hired my own crew."

Not for one minute did Dexter believe his father would resort to bribery, but he asked just the same. "Do you believe my father paid off the survey team you hired to falsify their findings?"

A loud sigh escaped Hank, and he aged ten years before Dexter's eyes. "No one's fault but my own for selling that land below market value. After J.W. and I signed the sales papers I got a letter in the mail from Pennyton's son. He said I'd gotten what I deserved." Hank's arthritic fingers clenched his kneecaps.

"I had a bad feeling about the survey so I drove over to the courthouse. That's when I found out J.W. had had one done, too, and it showed the gas deposits beneath the Lazy S. I put two and two together and figured out that bastard Frederick Pennyton had paid the survey company I hired to skewer the results."

"Didn't you take your suspicions to the sheriff and let him investigate?"

"I did. Sheriff Percy said there wasn't enough proof to point the finger at Frederick."

Dexter was relieved his father hadn't been involved in unethical business practices, but that didn't excuse him from taking advantage of his neighbor's misfortune. "Why didn't you confront my father and explain what happened?"

Hank's face turned red. "Pride's a nasty disease, son. Holding a grudge against J.W. was easier than admitting my own stupidity."

"That doesn't excuse my father. He knew the truth about the value of that land, yet he didn't—"

"No, son, he did." Hank cleared his throat. "When Sheriff Percy told J.W. about my suspicions that Pennyton's son had paid off the survey team but we didn't have enough proof, J.W. sent me another check."

Thank God his father had done the right thing.

"I returned the check."

"That money was rightfully yours."

"I wouldn't let your father pay for my mistakes."

"But that land will be worth a fortune when Walker taps into those gas wells."

"I reckon it doesn't matter who owns that land, seeing how my grandson's a Cody and my daughter's about to become one."

Yesterday Josie had been adamant that she'd wanted nothing to do with marrying Dusty. Gas wells forgotten, Dexter asked, "So Josie's decided to accept Dusty's proposal?"

"I didn't care much for Dusty when he and Josie dated in high school. Never could figure out what those two saw in each other." He motioned to Dexter. "Now you and Josie—that's a match I can see."

Surprised by Hank's honesty, Dexter said, "I'm not Matt's father."

"You've been more of a father to that boy in the past month than anyone else."

His chest tightened at the faith Hank had in him, but everything inside Dexter insisted that claiming Josie for his own would tear his family apart. "Dusty deserves a chance."

"A brush with death makes a man realize his years are numbered." Hank's eyes narrowed. "I'd like to see Josie and Matt stick around Markton."

"She will if she marries Dusty."

"There's only one man Josie would give up California for, and it's not the one coming out of the barn right now."

Dexter swallowed hard. Was he doing the right thing in not claiming Josie for his own? She deserved to be loved within an inch of her life, and Dexter was the only man who could do that—who already loved Josie to distraction.

He watched Dusty and Matt walk hand in hand. The boy chatted up a storm, and Dusty appeared genuinely interested in what Matt had to say. Father and son had found common ground.

"Mr. D!" Matt sprinted to the porch, leaving Dusty trailing behind him. The boy raced up the steps and jumped in Dexter's lap.

Dexter's heart turned to mush at the big blue eyes gazing up at him. He already felt like Matt's father and the thought of giving the boy over to Dusty made his chest ache. "What's up, buddy?"

"Dusty says he's a better roper than you."

"He did, huh?" Dexter stared at Dusty, who paused before the porch steps. Dexter tightened his hold on Matt, and Dusty looked away.

"I told my dad—" Matt tugged Dexter's shirtsleeve to get his attention "—that you put a saddle on Zeus, and my dad said you were the best whisper around."

"Whisperer," Dusty corrected.

"Yeah." Matt clasped Dexter's face between his little hands. "I'm gonna be a whisper just like you when I grow up." Matt frowned as he studied Dexter's face. He'd been too excited to notice the bruises until now. "Did a cow hurt you, too, Mr. D?"

"Yeah, buddy, but I'm okay."

Matt wrapped his arms around Dexter's neck and squeezed. "I don't want you to be hurt ever, Mr. D."

Dexter's eyes stung so damned bad he squeezed them shut before he embarrassed himself. When he finally blinked, Dusty wore a sad smile.

"My dad says you're gonna rodeo tomorrow. Can I come?"

Dexter glanced at Hank.

"Don't see why not," Hank said. "Be good for you to watch your daddy and your uncles compete."

"Can I rodeo, Grandpa?"

"You'll have to ask your mother about that."

"Okay." Matt slid off Dexter's lap and ran into the house.

"He's a great kid," Dusty said.

"He is." Hank leveled a pointed look at Dusty. "See that he stays that way."

"Yes, sir." Dusty turned to Dexter. "We'd better get another round of practice in."

"See you tomorrow, Hank." Dexter tipped his hat and followed Dusty to the truck.

Neither brother spoke a word the whole way home, each busy fighting their own demons.

Chapter Fourteen

The pungent smell of dung, worn leather and smoky barbecue assaulted Josie's nostrils and made her eyes water as she, Matt and her parents entered the arena at the Missoula Hoedown Rodeo Saturday afternoon. Hoping to avoid a confrontation with J.W. and Anne Cody, Josie had delayed finding their seats until just before the opening ceremony. Spectators, from all over Montana as well as other states, packed the arena eager to watch cowboys and cowgirls wrestle steers, bust broncs, tangle with bulls and rope calves.

Josie led the way to the cheap seats in the bleachers. The temperature hovered in the upper eighties and thankfully clouds had gathered in the sky, providing some relief from the heat. She stared with envy at the expensive seats located beneath a covered grandstand. Industrial-size fans circulated the air and misters kept fairgoers comfortable. Josie scanned the crowd, searching for J.W. and Anne Cody. She imagined their excitement at meeting their grandson today and hoped the reunion would go off without a hitch.

A flash of color caught her eye. *Anne*. Dressed in an aquamarine cowboy shirt with black fringe along the yoke and shoulders, the older woman looked elegant and every inch the matriarch of a wealthy ranching family. J.W. sat next to her clothed in traditional ranching garb—a Western shirt, bolo tie and blue jeans. Josie breathed a sigh of relief that the couple's gaze had skipped over her.

She hadn't gotten a wink of sleep the previous night—thoughts of Dexter stealing her peace. Why did she have to fall in love with such a stubborn man? He was determined to step aside so Dusty could step up.

What Dexter failed to take into consideration was that no amount of persuasion would convince her that marrying his twin was the right thing to do. Dusty didn't want marriage any more than Josie, and she'd gotten the impression he'd been relieved that she'd stood her ground and refused to marry him.

Matt's excitement was palpable. Thank goodness Josie's parents enjoyed listening to their grandson jabber nonstop, because she couldn't concentrate on anything but Dexter and the feeling that if she didn't do something drastic to change his mind about them, they'd both be making the biggest mistake of their lives.

Josie believed with every fiber of her being that Dexter was the man she was meant to be with for the rest of her life—the man she was meant to love.

A program hawker passed by and her father purchased one, then handed it to her. She scanned the list of events—Ellen would be the first of the Codys to compete. Bull riding followed barrel racing, then bronc busting, the chuck wagon races and lastly Dexter and Dusty's event—team roping.

"Ladies and gents, welcome to the Missoula Hoedown Rodeo!"

Music blared from the loudspeakers as a group of cowgirls carrying U.S. flags circled the arena on horseback. A young woman dressed from head to toe in red raced into the middle of the circle on a white gelding. She stopped in the center and dismounted, then approached a small stage.

"Please stand for the National Anthem sung by the Missoula Hoedown Rodeo Queen, Candy Morton."

Candy did a decent job singing the anthem, but Josie attributed the rousing applause that followed to the rodeo queen's curvaceous figure, big blond hair and skintight outfit.

Once the queen and her court left the arena, the crowd settled into their seats, and the announcer asked guests to bow their heads as he recited the famous Rodeo Cowboy's Prayer.

"Okay, folks, it's time for the barrel racing competition! In this event, the fastest time wins. If one of the cowgirls knocks a barrel down they'll be assessed a five-second penalty. But that ain't gonna happen, 'cause we've got the best barrel racers in the country competing today."

Josie had attempted barrel racing in high school, but had never managed to acquire the hang of controlling the horse around the turns. One bad spill and a broken thumb had been reason enough to quit the sport. While the first few cowgirls raced, Josie switched her attention to the opposite end of the arena, where stock contractors loaded bulls into the chutes. Each bull acted like a favorite family pet—until a cowboy sat on its back.

"We're down to our last cowgirl of the day, Ellen Cody." The cheers grew in volume—Ellen was a favorite among rodeo fans. "If the Cody name sounds familiar it's because the whole family's here today. Let's see if Ellen and her horse, Pepper, can give the family their first win. Sixteen point nine seconds is the time to beat."

"Matt, that cowgirl is your aunt Ellen." Josie pointed to Elly.

"Is she gonna win?"

"I hope so." Josie crossed her fingers and Matt copied her actions. A moment later Ellen and Pepper flew past the electric eye into the arena. Josie held her breath as Ellen turned the horse tightly around the first barrel. The crowd roared. Ellen circled the second barrel without incident, then guided Pepper around the third barrel, before racing toward the exit. The fans' eyes shifted to the clock above the JumboTron.

"Sixteen point seven seconds! Ellen Cody and her horse, Pepper, win first place!" When the crowd quieted, the announcer added, "Time will tell if the Cody brothers can match their sister's performance."

Josie spied Dexter walking toward Ellen. His sexy cowboy swagger spawned heated memories of a certain mechanical bull. Dexter hugged his sister and they spoke for a moment. Then his eyes searched the stands. Was he looking for her? When he glanced at Josie's section she popped out of her seat.

I'm right here, Dex. Josie's heart thudded in disappointment when he turned away.

Rodeo clowns cartwheeled into the arena and entertained the fans while the cowboys prepared for the bull-riding event, but Josie only had eyes for Dexter. She followed his movements behind the chutes, wishing he'd stop and search for her again.

Dexter wove through the throng of competitors toward his brother Jesse, who was engaged in a heated discussion with Mark Hansen. If Jesse's and Mark's expressions were any indication, the conversation was far from friendly.

Josie's father nudged her arm. "Mark Hansen and Jesse Cody are fierce competitors," he said.

As long as Josie could remember, Mark and Jesse had never liked each other. They'd both ridden for Riverside High's rodeo team, but Jesse had been the better of the two. Josie hated to think the men were still at odds after all these years. Then she considered her dad and J.W. and admitted intense rivalries were the nature of the sport.

"Looks like Hansen's getting ganged up on," her father said.

Walker, Ellen and Dusty had joined Dexter to lend Jesse their support. Josie sympathized with Mark— the guy didn't stand a chance when the Cody siblings banded together. Josie checked the grandstands. J.W. and Anne watched the exchange with worried expressions on their faces.

"The town's split because of having two good bull riders," her father said. "The way I figure, no matter who wins the NFR this December, Markton comes out a winner."

Right then Jesse shoved Mark and he stumbled backward. Mark raised his arm to punch his competitor, but Janie Hansen stepped between the two bull riders. The short, dark-haired, curvaceous woman glared at her brother. Nicki Sable joined the group, her ire directed at her longtime friend Jesse. Both men knew when they were outmatched and backed down.

"Ladies and gents, it's time for a little bull riding!"

The crowd roared as the clowns exited the arena and scenes of bull rides from previous rodeos flashed across the JumboTron. "The stakes are high for two of our contestants. Jesse Cody and Mark Hansen are tied for first place in the standings. Both bull buckers want to make it to Vegas at the end of the year, and a win today means sole possession of first place."

"My bet's on Mark," Josie's father said.

"Why?"

"Hansen's got a chip on his shoulder. He wants it more."

"What kind of chip?" She didn't know a whole lot about Mark except that he grew up dirt-poor—but then most of Markton was poor compared to the Codys.

Her father didn't have time to explain before the announcer proceeded with the introductions. "First up is Bo Cutter. Bo's an Oklahoma boy and sits in tenth place in the standings. He's ridin' Gator!"

Josie paid scant attention to the bull ride; instead she kept track of Dexter's movements. He patted Jesse on the back, and the brothers bowed their heads in private conversation. She wished she'd had a brother or sister to take her side in an argument no matter if she was right or wrong. For the first time she saw the Codys not as a threat to her son but as a blessing.

Matt would grow up surrounded by family, who would protect him and support his endeavors in life. Yes, J.W. and Anne would probably spoil Matt rotten—not with fire trucks or toy trains but with real-live horses, F-150s and vacations around the world. Josie couldn't compete with that, but she'd do her best to raise her son to be humble and generous with the wealth the Codys bequeathed to him.

Her father nudged her side. "Mark's up next."

"Folks, Mark Hansen from Markton, Wyoming, has drawn Dirt Devil. Look over at chute number five. Dirt Devil's already pickin' a fight with Hansen."

The bull rammed his side against the rails. Mark raised his leg in the nick of time, sparing himself serious injury.

"Dirt Devil's a head thrower, which means he's gonna try to hit the cowboy with his horns while he's buckin'." The fans booed the bull.

The gate opened and Dirt Devil shot into the arena. As the announcer predicted, the bull flung his head back in an attempt to injure his rider. Mark managed to keep his seat and his face away from the deadly horns. Eight seconds lasted a lifetime. When the buzzer sounded Mark remained seated on the bull and the arena exploded with applause. The bullfighters rushed Dirt Devil, and Mark jumped to safety, then stumbled toward the rails.

"Hansen's earned an 82! Good enough to take over first place. Now getting ready in chute eight is Hansen's rival, Jesse Cody. The cowboy's drawn a money bull. If Cody lasts eight seconds on Grim Reaper, he'll take home a little pocket change!"

Josie watched Jesse wrap the bull rope around his hand, then the gate opened and Grim Reaper catapulted into the air. Men shouted. Women screamed. She wondered if Jesse heard the commotion, or if he blocked out all the noise. The bull bucked so hard it looked as if

Jesse's arm might rip from its socket. His pristine white hat flew off and landed beneath the bull's hooves where the animal promptly stomped it flat.

Six...seven... The buzzer sounded and Jesse looked for an escape route. When all four of the bull's legs hit the ground at once, Jesse flung himself off the animal. Grim Reaper twisted left, almost hooking Jesse in the head. When the bull regained his balance, he charged.

The bullfighters closed in, but Grim Reaper wouldn't be deterred—his rage focused solely on Jesse. The roar in the arena dropped several decibels. Josie held her breath when Dexter climbed the chute and threw one leg over the top rail, poised to come to his brother's aid if need be. Once again Dexter proved why Josie loved him so much—his loyalty to family went beyond anything she'd ever known.

She wanted that love and loyalty for herself.

Jesse had no chance to gain his footing before the bull struck his backside, sending him sprawling into the dirt. The crowd gasped, then the bull changed direction and went after one of the bullfighters. Jesse limped to safety among the roar of fans, Dexter right there with a helping hand.

"Well, folks, I gotta feelin' that was our ride of the day."

The crowd's applause increased when an 85 flashed on the JumboTron. "Jesse Cody is our first place winner! Ti yi yippee-yippee-yay!"

"Did Uncle Jesse win, Mom?" Matt asked.

"He sure did, honey." Josie looked across the arena and discovered Anne Cody's gaze glued to Matt. The longing on the older woman's face brought tears to

Josie's eyes. Anne's attention shifted to Josie, and the older woman flashed a hesitant smile. Josie smiled back.

She considered escorting Matt around the arena to meet his grandparents but decided Dusty should be the one to introduce them. Right then Anne nudged J.W. and pointed in Josie's direction. J.W.'s stern expression changed to wonderment when he spotted Matt. She supposed even from this distance there was no mistaking that Matt was Dusty's son.

Worry about how Matt would react to meeting his new grandparents kept Josie's mind occupied during the bronc-riding competition. By the time the final cowboy had competed, she'd decided she'd fretted for nothing and forced herself to relax.

"Folks, we got a special treat today before we move on to team roping—the final event of the afternoon. Get ready for the pony chuck races."

Rodeo workers set up the barrels for the race. Two miniature chuck wagons would compete at one time.

"Wait until you see this, Matt," she said when the first pair of wagons came into view. The drivers and their partners wore Western shirts, which matched the color of their wagons—robin-egg blue and apricot.

"Folks, this here race is called Hell's Half Mile!" The announcer chuckled. "When the race begins, the driver's assistants are gonna climb over the seat and stow all the pots and pans hanging on the cross bow in that there cupboard in the back. The cowboy who packs up the most dishes before their wagon crosses the finish line wins."

A gun blast rent the air and the wagons took off, kicking up a dust storm. One cowboy crawled over the bench seat and lost his balance, but managed to hang on when his legs swung out alongside the wagon. He flung himself over the side, knocking his head on a cast-iron skillet in the process.

As the wagons made the tight turns, pots and pans swayed on the cross bow and the cowboys ducked to avoid getting clobbered. On the far side of the arena, Dexter and Dusty made their way to the calf chutes.

You're not a quitter, Josie. Her heart demanded she try one more time to get it through Dexter's thick skull that they were meant to be together. If no amount of pleading changed his mind, then Dexter wasn't the man she believed he was and she'd be better off without him.

"I'm going to speak with Dexter." With single-minded determination, Josie moved through the crowd.

DEXTER AND DUSTY STROLLED toward the steer chutes where Ricky and Slim held the reins for Uno and Digger. The ranch hands had made the four-and-a-half-hour drive up to Missoula earlier in the day with the horses while the family had opted for air travel. Dusty had extended an invitation to the Charles family to join them, but Josie had declined the offer—Dexter suspected Hank had refused to board his nemesis's private plane. Dexter hoped that sharing a grandson would convince the old coots to bury the hatchet and become friends.

"Good luck," Ricky said when the twins approached. Slim handed Digger's reins to Dexter, then the two ranch hands retreated to the stands to watch the event.

Dexter checked his rigging. "You ready?"

"I'm always ready." Dusty tipped his hat and flashed his Hollywood smile at a passing female. Once the lady disappeared, Dusty became all businesslike. "Wait for me to turn the steer before you throw your rope."

If Dexter threw his rope too soon they'd earn a cross fire penalty, which would take them right out of contention. Granted, Dusty was the more talented athlete of the twins, but, irritable from lack of sleep, Dexter warned, "You make sure you don't break the barrier."

Dusty snorted. "Hell, I never break the barrier."

True enough. "You ever get tired of thinking so highly of yourself?" Dexter bit the inside of his cheek to keep from smiling. Baiting his brother kept his mind off Josie. He had hoped to run into her and Matt before the team roping event, but no such luck. He wondered if perhaps she and her parents had decided against making the long drive to Missoula.

A handful of rodeo groupies called Dusty's name. "Afternoon, ladies." The females giggled, their sashaying hips advertising *I'm yours for the taking.*

"I don't get it," Dexter said.

"Get what?"

"How you can flirt with women after you proposed to Josie."

"Quit thinking about Josie. Concentrate on our event. We're not letting Jesse and Elly show us up today."

Unbelievable. "With everything that's happened over the past few weeks all you can think about is winning?" Dexter shook his head. "You're screwed up, man."

"You're more messed up than I am."

"Yeah, well, I'm not the one who has a son."

"So it's my fault that Josie never told me?"

Dexter couldn't blame Dusty for that, but right now he didn't care about trivial details. "You treated Josie no better than the rodeo bimbos you've hooked up with."

"Exactly what do you find so offensive about the way I treat bimbos?"

"You jump into bed with them the first chance you get."

"Yeah, like you'd turn down a little mattress dancing if the opportunity came your way?" Dusty's eyes lit with laughter.

"Can't we have a serious discussion just once?"

"You want serious? I can do serious." The mirth drained from Dusty's eyes, and he leveled a sober stare at Dexter. "How about this for serious—you're in love with Josie, but you won't admit it."

The knot that had formed in Dexter's gut the moment his brother had returned from Canada twisted tighter, but before Dexter could catch his breath his brother went on the attack.

"You wanted Josie in high school. But you never fought for her."

"You're right." Dexter had been head over heels for Josie, yet he'd stood aside while Dusty worked his magic on Josie. "But I was friends with Josie before you two ever dated. So if you knew I liked her, then why didn't you keep your distance and let me ask Josie out first?" Shoot, his brother could have had any girl in high school, yet he picked the one Dexter had wanted.

"Because…" Dusty kicked a clump of dirt, then looked Dexter in the eye. "Because I'd heard gossip that Josie liked me. Not you."

"So you asked her out first to spare me the humiliation of being turned down?"

Dusty shrugged. "I figured once Josie and I dated a couple of times she'd see that I wasn't the right twin for her and she'd give you a chance."

"Didn't work out that way," Dexter said.

"I never expected Josie and I to hit it off and...well, the rest is history." He blew out a heavy breath. "I'm sorry, Dex."

The Codys were a proud family and the word *sorry* wasn't spoken lightly. "I forgive you."

"Good. Now I'm gonna ask the questions. Aren't you tired of always doing the honorable thing? Tired of putting family first? Following Dad's commands?" Dusty paused, then added, "Aren't you tired of never going after what *you* want?"

"Family comes first." The words almost choked Dexter.

"Not all the time." Dusty clasped Dexter's shoulder. "Love. Real love trumps family. The love you feel for Josie is worth sacrificing your honor for."

Longing for Josie burned in Dexter's veins. "You really don't have any feelings for Josie?" Dexter's heart braced itself.

"I care about her because she's the mother of my son. Her happiness is important to me. If you can make her happy, Dex, then that's what I want for her."

Don't you get it? Dusty is doing right by Josie by telling you to go after her. Dusty knows you're the best man for her.

Dexter feared once he spoke his feelings out loud there would be no turning back. No taking the high road. No putting family first. "You're right. I'm in love with Josie."

Dusty grinned. "No shit, loser."

Dexter punched his brother in the arm. "Knock it off." He sobered. "I should have fought you for Josie in high school."

Dusty's expression sobered. "Yep, you should have."

"I'm tired of giving up what *I* want," Dexter said.

"So… What do you intend to do about it?"

Dexter grabbed Dusty by the shirt collar and threatened, "Josie's mine. You stay the hell away from her, you hear."

"Loud and clear." Dusty grinned, then pointed over Dexter's shoulder.

Dexter spun and found Josie standing a few yards away. His heart tumbled at the sight of her. He walked to her side and cupped her face. "I love you. And I want you, Josie. I want you for *me*."

Her eyes shimmered with tears. "I love you, too, Dex."

Dexter bent his head and kissed her. Slow and soft, he pledged his love to her, and when they came up for air they were surrounded by family—his and Josie's. There was never a better time to propose.

Clasping Josie's hand, Dexter went down on one knee. "I love you, Josie Charles. I want to be your husband, your lover and help you raise Matt." He placed his cowboy hat over his heart. "Will you marry me?"

Tears dribbled down Josie's cheeks and darned if she could stop them.

"Mom's crying, Grandma," Matt said.

"That's because she's very happy, dear," Phyllis Charles said.

Matt walked to his mother's side. "If my mom marries you, Mr. D, does that mean I'm gonna have two dads?" Matt glanced at Dusty.

"Yes, it does. Is that okay with you?" Dexter said.

Matt smiled. "Yeah, that's okay." He tugged Josie's sleeve. "You can marry Mr. D, Mom."

Josie caressed Dexter's cheek. "Yes, I'll marry you, Dexter."

Dexter stood and swung Josie around amid hoots and hollers from the family. After he set her on her feet, he held out his hand to Matt. Together they approached Dexter's parents.

"Matt, this is your grandma and grandpa Cody. Mom and Dad, this is Matt."

Anne Cody's eyes misted as she swept a hand over Matt's hair. "You're as handsome as your fathers." Matt preened under the attention.

"Since you're a Cody, young man, you'll need to be thinking about what rodeo event you want to compete in." J.W. engaged in a stare-down with Hank. "Your grandpa Charles was a world-class bronc rider. We could use a good bronc rider in the family."

Josie wanted to cry at the olive branch J.W. had offered her father. Josie's dad chimed in. "Or, Matt, you might consider riding bulls. Your uncle Jesse's the best there is."

Dusty moved next to Dexter and mumbled, "Thank God you came to your senses."

"Shut up, Dusty. There was no way I was gonna let you get the girl this time."

Dusty nudged Dexter's arm.

"What is it?"

"Hansen. He's been standing over there watching us like a lost calf." The bull rider hovered behind the chutes, his expression tormented.

Dexter glanced at his father, who stared at Hansen with the same damned expression on his face. What the hell was going on between his father and Mark Hansen? There wasn't time to find out—the announcer kicked off the team roping event. Josie flung her arms around Dexter's neck and kissed him good luck.

"Where's my kiss?" Dusty grinned.

Dexter tugged his brother's arm. "C'mon, Casanova—time to compete."

The Codys and the Charleses watched Dexter and Dusty from behind the chutes. As soon as they'd roped the calf, Matt announced, "I wanna do that. Just like my dads."

J.W. eyed Josie. "You're gonna need a partner for team roping, Grandson. You'd best tell your mother to get working on a brother or two for you."

Josie blushed, her heart lighter than it had been in days, months, years. Becoming part of the Cody clan wouldn't be without conflict—families who loved deeply also fought deeply.

From the beginning Josie had been destined to become a Cody, and she and Matt were finally with the right Cody. *Dexter.*

Epilogue

"Are you sure you're not disappointed that we didn't have a big wedding?" Dexter asked Josie three days after the Missoula Hoedown Rodeo.

Josie snuggled deeper into his lap. After their first full day as Mr. and Mrs. Cody, they sat in a rocking chair on her parents' porch watching the sun set. "Our wedding was beautiful. Your mom did an incredible job with the decorations." They'd been married by a justice of the peace in the backyard of Anne and J.W.'s home. The wedding was intimate—only family and close friends had been invited. Following the reception, Josie's parents had taken off for the airport. Dexter had surprised his in-laws with tickets for an Alaskan cruise. Josie's father had insisted Dexter and Josie go on the cruise for their honeymoon, but Dexter hinted that he had something special planned for Josie, Matt and him in the near future.

Her father had relented and Josie and Dexter were honeymooning at the Lazy S ranch house. Matt was staying with Anne and J.W. so Josie and Dexter could—in J.W.'s words—"work on a brother or sister for Matt."

"Matt called when you were in the barn," Josie said. "Is he lonely?"

"Hardly. He had to tell me he was getting a new horse but it wouldn't be born until next spring."

"If you want, I'll tell Mom and Dad to ease up on the gifts." Dexter nuzzled her neck and she shivered.

"I don't stand a chance of stopping your parents from spoiling Matt rotten, but promise me Matt's going to grow up and be just like you, Dex—an honorable, caring man."

"Don't forget persistent like his mother."

She sighed when Dexter kissed her.

"I almost let you walk away from me, Josie. If you hadn't—"

"You would have come after me. We were meant to be together."

"I hope your dad doesn't regret gifting us the five hundred acres that borders my family's ranch."

"We're all one family now, Dex. Besides, Dad's tired. He loves the Lazy S but he's too worn-out to raise cattle. He's ready to retire and watch his grandchildren grow up. And he likes the idea that we'll build our own house close by."

"He told me that if anything happens to him he wants Matt to have the Lazy S."

"Dad told me that, too, and I promised him you and I would keep this ranch in the family." Josie and her father had had a long discussion about the past. She admitted she was disappointed in her father for allowing her to believe that J.W. had swindled him out of valuable land. How different all their lives might have been had Josie not been afraid to tell Dusty he'd gotten her pregnant all those years ago. The past was better left in the past, and Josie was relieved J.W. appeared willing to mend fences with her father. As J.W. had told Josie and Dexter, "No matter how long you live, life goes by fast." Neither Cody grandparent wanted to waste a minute fighting when they could spend that time with their grandchildren.

Josie giggled.

"What's so funny?" Dexter asked.

"Just remembering the look of relief on Dusty's face after we both said I do."

Dexter chuckled. "I think he was worried one of us would back out at the last minute."

"Dusty's a good guy. One day he'll find his perfect match."

"Time will tell if there's a lady who can tame my brother's wild ways."

"Dex?"

"What?"

"My wedding present to you should arrive by the end of the week."

"Oh, yeah? A new cowboy hat? Boots?"

"Nope. As a matter of fact you won't be needing any clothes to use my gift."

His eyebrows rose, and Josie couldn't keep a secret for the life of her. She removed a piece of paper from her jean pocket and handed it to him.

He stared, then hooted. After he wiped his eyes he read the advertisement. "Rockin' M Bucking Machines—Home of Brutus the Bull." Dexter grinned. "You bought a mechanical bull for me?"

She batted her eyelashes. "For us."

"Life with you sure won't be dull, Josie." His kiss gave her a teasing glimpse of what she could expect once Dexter's gift arrived. "This means we'll have to install a lock on the door to the back room in the barn," he said when they came up for air.

"And hang a Do Not Disturb sign."

"What will your parents say when they catch us sneaking into the barn late at night?"

"As long as another grandchild results from our late-night bull-riding lessons, they won't say a thing." Josie clasped Dexter's face between her hands. "Now kiss me, and sweep me off my feet."

"Yes, ma'am."

* * * * *

We hope you're enjoying the Cody Family saga!
Watch for more stories featuring these men
and women of the West.
WALKER: The Rodeo Legend (June 2010)
DUSTY: Wild Cowboy (August 2010)
MARK: Secret Cowboy (September 2010)
ELLY: Cowgirl Bride (October 2010)
JESSE: Merry Christmas, Cowboy (November 2010)

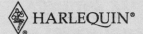

HARLEQUIN®

COMING NEXT MONTH

Available August 10, 2010

#1317 BABY BOMBSHELL
Babies & Bachelors USA
Lisa Ruff

#1318 DUSTY: WILD COWBOY
The Codys: The First Family of Rodeo
Cathy McDavid

#1319 THE MOMMY PROPOSAL
The Lone Star Dads Club
Cathy Gillen Thacker

#1320 HIS HIRED BABY
Safe Harbor Medical
Jacqueline Diamond

HARCNM0710

REQUEST YOUR FREE BOOKS!
2 FREE NOVELS PLUS 2 FREE GIFTS!

HARLEQUIN®

American ★ Romance®

Love, Home & Happiness!

YES! Please send me 2 FREE Harlequin® American Romance® novels and my 2 FREE gifts (gifts are worth about $10). After receiving them, if I don't wish to receive any more books, I can return the shipping statement marked "cancel." If I don't cancel, I will receive 4 brand-new novels every month and be billed just $4.24 per book in the U.S. or $4.99 per book in Canada. That's a saving of at least 15% off the cover price! It's quite a bargain! Shipping and handling is just 50¢ per book.* I understand that accepting the 2 free books and gifts places me under no obligation to buy anything. I can always return a shipment and cancel at any time. Even if I never buy another book from Harlequin, the two free books and gifts are mine to keep forever.

154/354 HDN E5LG

Name _____ (PLEASE PRINT) _____

Address _____ Apt. # _____

City _____ State/Prov. _____ Zip/Postal Code _____

Signature (if under 18, a parent or guardian must sign)

Mail to the **Harlequin Reader Service:**
IN U.S.A.: P.O. Box 1867, Buffalo, NY 14240-1867
IN CANADA: P.O. Box 609, Fort Erie, Ontario L2A 5X3

Not valid for current subscribers to Harlequin® American Romance® books.

Want to try two free books from another line?
Call 1-800-873-8635 or visit www.morefreebooks.com.

* Terms and prices subject to change without notice. Prices do not include applicable taxes. N.Y. residents add applicable sales tax. Canadian residents will be charged applicable provincial taxes and GST. Offer not valid in Quebec. This offer is limited to one order per household. All orders subject to approval. Credit or debit balances in a customer's account(s) may be offset by any other outstanding balance owed by or to the customer. Please allow 4 to 6 weeks for delivery. Offer available while quantities last.

Your Privacy: Harlequin is committed to protecting your privacy. Our Privacy Policy is available online at www.eHarlequin.com or upon request from the Reader Service. From time to time we make our lists of customers available to reputable third parties who may have a product or service of interest to you. If you would prefer we not share your name and address, please check here. ☐

Help us get it right—We strive for accurate, respectful and relevant communications. To clarify or modify your communication preferences, visit us at www.ReaderService.com/consumerschoice.

HAR10R

HARLEQUIN®

A Romance

FOR EVERY MOOD™

Spotlight on

Heart & Home

Heartwarming romances
where love can happen
right when you least expect it.

See the next page to enjoy a sneak peek
from Harlequin® American Romance®,
a Heart and Home series.

Five hunky Texas single fathers—five stories from
Cathy Gillen Thacker's LONE STAR DADS *miniseries.*
Here's an excerpt from the latest, THE MOMMY PROPOSAL
from Harlequin American Romance.

"I hear you work miracles," Nate Hutchinson drawled. Brooke Mitchell had just stepped into his lavishly appointed office in downtown Fort Worth, Texas.

"Sometimes, I do." Brooke smiled and took the sexy financier's hand in hers, shook it briefly.

"Good." Nate looked her straight in the eye. "Because I'm in need of a home makeover—fast. The son of an old friend is coming to live with me."

She was still tingling from the feel of his warm palm. "Temporarily or permanently?"

"If all goes according to plan, I'll adopt Landry by summer's end."

Brooke had heard the founder of Nate Hutchinson Financial Services was eligible, wealthy and generous to a fault. She hadn't known he was in the market for a family, but she supposed she shouldn't be surprised. But Brooke had figured a man as successful and handsome as Nate would want one the old-fashioned way. *Not that this was any of her business...*

"So what's the child like?" she asked crisply, trying not to think how the marine-blue of Nate's dress shirt deepened the hue of his eyes.

"I don't know." Nate took a seat behind his massive antique mahogany desk. He relaxed against the smooth leather of the chair. "I've never met him."

"Yet you've invited this kid to live with you permanently?"

"It's complicated. But I'm sure it's going to be fine."

Obviously Nate Hutchinson knew as little about teenage

HAREXP0810

boys as he did about decorating. But that wasn't her problem. Finding a way to do the assignment without getting the least bit emotionally involved was.

Find out how a young boy brings Nate and Brooke together in THE MOMMY PROPOSAL, coming August 2010 from Harlequin American Romance.

HAREXP0810

Fan favourite

Molly O'Keefe

brings readers a brand-new miniseries

Beginning with

The Temptation of Savannah O'Neill

Escaping her family's reputation was all Savannah O'Neill ever wanted. Then Matt Woods shows up posing as a simple handyman, and she can see there's much more to him than meets the eye. However tempted to get beneath his surface, she knows that uncovering his secrets could expose her own. But as Matt begins to open himself up to Savannah, that's when the trouble really begins....

Available August 2010 wherever books are sold.

HARLEQUIN
Ambassadors

Want to share your passion for reading Harlequin® Books?

Become a Harlequin Ambassador!

Harlequin Ambassadors are a group of passionate and well-connected readers who are willing to share their joy of reading Harlequin® books with family and friends.

You'll be sent all the tools you need to spark great conversation, including free books!

All we ask is that you share the romance with your friends and family!

You'll also be invited to have a say in new book ideas and exchange opinions with women just like you!

To see if you qualify* to be a Harlequin Ambassador, please visit www.HarlequinAmbassadors.com.

*Please note that not everyone who applies to be a Harlequin Ambassador will qualify. For more information please visit www.HarlequinAmbassadors.com.

Thank you for your participation.

BAP09BPA